ONE MAN
TO ANOTHER

Francis Durbridge

WILLIAMS & WHITING

Cover design by Timo Schroeder

9781915887092

Williams & Whiting (Publishers)
15 Chestnut Grove, Hurstpierpoint,
West Sussex, BN6 9SS

Titles by Francis Durbridge published by Williams & Whiting

Also published by Williams & Whiting:
Francis Durbridge : The Complete Guide
By Melvyn Barnes

INTRODUCTION

Francis Durbridge (1912-98) began his career as a writer of sketches, stories and plays for BBC radio from 1933. They were mostly light entertainments, including libretti for musical comedies, but a talent for crime fiction became evident in his early radio plays *Murder in the Midlands* (1934) and *Murder in the Embassy* (1937).

In the late 1930s he thought about creating a radio detective called Mark Conway, but soon changed his mind and settled finally for the dream team of novelist/detective Paul Temple and his wife Steve. Durbridge's radio serial *Send for Paul Temple* was first broadcast from 8 April to 27 May 1938, and proved so successful that more Temple cases followed for some thirty years and resulted in an impressive UK and European fanbase. While today his name remains firmly associated with Paul Temple, it might surprise many to learn that in the 1940s Durbridge also created radio detectives called Anthony Sherwood (1940), Johnny Cordell (1941), Amanda Smith (1941), Gail Carlton (1943), Michael Starr (1944), André d'Arnell (1944) and Johnny Washington (1949), and that he even wrote a radio serial featuring the legendary Sexton Blake (1940).

But perhaps at this point, for those not entirely familiar with Durbridge's work, it might be helpful to show the extent of his multi-media career. He wrote for BBC radio from 1933 to 1968, but while continuing his radio career in 1952 he launched a parallel series of BBC television serials (not featuring the Temples) that attracted sizeable audiences until 1980. Overlapping again, from 1971 he provided theatre audiences with nine expertly crafted and convoluted stage thrillers including *Suddenly at Home*, *Murder with Love* and *House Guest*. And for over twenty years he licensed his radio character Paul Temple as the subject of a syndicated newspaper strip that was published daily from 11 December 1950 until 1 May 1971 in the *London Evening News* and for various periods in many other UK and overseas newspapers.

There is no doubt that *Send for Paul Temple* established Francis Durbridge's reputation and made his name synonymous with an icon of twentieth-century radio, and he must have recognised the significance of this first Paul Temple case. So given that Durbridge later proved to have been a consummate recycler of his most successful plots, it is hardly surprising that over the years *Send for Paul Temple* was re-written in various forms.

Firstly it was novelised (John Long, June 1938), co-authored with John Thewes, and this was also published in France as *La Bande des oiseaux noirs* (The Band of Black Birds) and in the Netherlands as *Paul Vlaanderen en de ruitenboer* (Paul Vlaanderen and the Jack of Diamonds). In the UK, newspaper advertisements described it as "the novel of the thriller that created a BBC fan-mail record" and it was made Book of the Month by the Crime Book Society.

Just a few years later, *Send for Paul Temple* was adapted by Durbridge as a stage play. It was performed in Birmingham (1943) and Wolverhampton (1944), and combined elements of his second radio serial *Paul Temple and the Front Page Men*. Then came the cinema film *Send for Paul Temple* (Butchers/Nettlefold, 1946), with a screenplay by John Argyle and Durbridge, which was also released in the USA as *Mystery of the Green Finger* and *The Green Finger*, in Germany as *Der Grüne Finger*, in Austria as *Die Todesfalle* (The Deathtrap), in France as *L'Auberge des tueurs* (The Inn of Killers) and in Denmark as *Den grønne finger*.

The saga of *Send for Paul Temple* was far from over, however, and its next manifestation had a rather unusual origin. On BBC radio from 12 August to 30 September 1949 a series of eight thirty-minute plays by Durbridge was broadcast under the title *Johnny Washington Esquire*, telling of a young American in London who turned the tables with barely legal coups at the expense of social parasites and underworld villains. It provided the basis of the novel *Beware of Johnny Washington* (John Long, April 1951), and one can only speculate that this spinoff was prompted by the popularity of the radio series and that the character had attracted fans among the listening public at a time when radio was the principal medium of home entertainment. But in this novel the only connection with the radio series was Johnny Washington himself – and probably because the radio short stories would not have made a novel, plus the likelihood that Durbridge was too busy with his other radio work to produce a timely and original Washington novel, *Beware of Johnny Washington* was a reworking of *Send for Paul Temple*. It kept to the main plot quite closely, but introduced new characters and subplots, and Washington instead of Temple joined forces with Verity Glyn instead of Steve Trent in the hunt for her brother's killer.

So what of *One Man to Another*, the typescript of which was recently discovered? It is another spinoff from *Send for Paul Temple*, but in this case the principal characters are Harry Denver and Diana Stone. It might perhaps have been intended for translation overseas or for publication in the USA, but this is speculation and there is no evidence that *One Man to Another* was ever published until now. To narrow down the date it was written, there is one small clue - in Chapter Seven there is mention of the Beatles, which means it must be post-1960 and therefore at least ten years after the publication of *Beware of Johnny Washington*.

This series of books published by Williams and Whiting transcribes a substantial number of Francis Durbridge's original typescripts. Many came to fruition as radio broadcasts, television serials and cinema movies, but some never made it into final production. Each one nevertheless displays Durbridge's mastery of plot construction and epitomises his trademark twists and turns, which will be a revelation to present day readers.

Melvyn Barnes
Author of *Francis Durbridge: The Complete Guide* (Williams & Whiting 2018)

CHAPTER ONE

"Another gelignite job," said Chief-Inspector Rymer, folding his arms and gazing moodily through the tall window of the Assistant Commissioner's office.

"Ten thousand pounds' worth of diamonds," added Superintendent Falconer in a worried tone. "Gloucester this time – we never know where they'll turn up next."

The Assistant Commissioner, Sir Richard McKendrick, pulled a stack of variously coloured folders towards him and selected a grey one. For a minute or two he thumbed over the papers in silence, while his subordinates eyed each other a trifle uncomfortably and waited for him to speak.

They watched him turning over one report after another, scanning them briefly, and stopping twice to make a pencilled note on the pad at his elbow. Meanwhile, the cigarette he had been smoking burnt slowly on the ashtray beside him.

A man in his late fifties, Sir Richard had attained his present position by a reputation for his capacity to digest facts rapidly and methodically and, having done so, to reach a quick decision which usually proved to be the right one.

The smoke from the chief's cigarette tickled Falconer's nose and he felt a sudden craving to light one himself, but he would not dare to do so without Sir Richard's invitation. There was an air of discipline about the plainly furnished office which one did not associate with tea-drinking and cigarettes. When you went to see Sir Richard you gave him your information, received his instructions, and left to put them into operation.

However, the gelignite robberies were in a class of their own on a scale that had not been encountered at the Yard for some years. A lorry load of gelignite which had been despatched to the scene of some mining operations in Cornwall had never arrived at its destination. The driver was discovered lying senseless at the side of the road in the early hours of the morning. All he remembered was climbing into his cab after calling at an all-night pull-up near Taunton and receiving a blow on the head which resulted in slight concussion. He had not even caught a glimpse of his assailant.

A week later the safe at a large super-cinema at Norwich was blown open with gelignite, and the week's takings, amounting to about one thousand five hundred pounds, were stolen. This was presumably in the nature of a try-out, for the delignate gang almost immediately went after bigger game. They began with a jewellers' safe in Birmingham, which yielded over five thousand pounds' worth of diamonds, pearls, and platinum settings. After Birmingham came Leicester, Sheffield, Oldham, and Shrewsbury. The aggregate value of the stolen goods was now in the region of five figures.

The Assistant Commissioner looked up from the report of the raid on the Gloucester jewellers, which he had been scanning carefully. "What about this night watchman?" he inquired.

"I'm afraid he's dead, sir," replied Falconer. "He was pretty heavily chloroformed, and according to the doctor his heart was in a bad state to stand up to any sudden shock."

Sir Richard frowned. "This is getting extremely serious," he murmured. "We shall have the papers playing it up worse than ever; then some damn fool will be asking a question in the House. Was the night watchman above board?"

Falconer shook his head. "I'm afraid not, sir. He'd only been with the firm about a month. He joined them under the name of Brookfield, but we soon found he had a long record as Wilfred Hiller, alias Burns. Everything from petty thefts to smash and grab."

"H'm! He might have been part of the set-up," grunted Sir Richard. "Pity they gave him an overdose …"

"It could have been one way to make sure he didn't talk – and to avoid paying him his cut," Rymer pointed out quietly.

Sir Richard nodded. "Who was in charge down there?"

"Inspector Bowen had already arrived when we got there – you remember we recalled him for the Special Branch to work on the gelignite jobs," replied Falconer. "He was questioning the Constable who discovered the robbery, a young man named Roscoe. Roscoe's only been in the Force two years but he's got quite a good record. He was apparently passing the jewellers on his beat and he noticed that the side door was open a couple of inches, so he went in to investigate."

"What about fingerprints?"

"Nothing we can trace, except the night watchman's, and they were nowhere near the safe," replied Falconer. "It was the same on all the other jobs. There's somebody running the outfit who really knows his way round."

Sir Richard shrugged and went on reading, a tiny furrow deepening between his eyebrows and his lips tightening into a thin line. "What did Bowen have to say?" he inquired at length.

Rymer smiled. "He didn't seem to know whether he was coming or going. Talked about a large criminal organisation – I think he's been meeting too many international spies."

A note of contempt in Rymer's voice prompted McKendrick to ask: "Then you don't think it is a criminal organisation?"

Rymer shook his head most decisively, a flicker of a grin around his thin mouth. "We're always reading about these big criminal set-ups," he said sarcastically, "but I've been with the police here and abroad for over fifteen years without coming across a sign of any really elaborate organisation. Crooks don't work that way; it's every man for himself and to hell with the one who's caught! Of course, we had the race-

3

course gangs a few years back, but that was different – not what you'd call scientifically planned crime. If you ask me, these jobs have been pulled by a little bunch of old lags."

Sir Richard swung round in his chair and stubbed out his cigarette. "What do you think, Falconer?" he demanded.

The Superintendent glanced across at his colleague and shifted uncomfortably in his chair. "I'm afraid I don't agree with Rymer, Sir Richard," he admitted at last. The Inspector looked startled for a moment and appeared to be about to make some comment, but he changed his mind, and Falconer went on, "I thought the same as Rymer for some time, but I've come to the conclusion this last week or so that these jobs are being planned to the last detail by some mentality far and away above that of the average crook."

McKendrick gave no sign as to whether he was impressed by this argument, other than making a brief note on his pad. "Did you see the night watchman before he died?" he asked.

Falconer nodded. "Yes, sir. He was in pretty bad shape, of course, and I thought he wouldn't be able to say anything. But the doctor gave him an injection and he seemed to recover consciousness."

"Well, what did he say?" urged McKendrick with a note of impatience in his tone.

The Superintendent rubbed his hands rather nervously. "I couldn't be quite sure, sir," he replied dubiously, "but it sounded to me rather like 'Grey Moose'."

There was the sound of a suppressed chuckle from Rymer, but the Assistant Commissioner was quickly turning through his file. "Here we are," he said suddenly. "A report on the Oldham case – you remember Smoky Pearce died rather mysteriously soon after? He was run over by a lorry – found by a Constable on the Preston Road – there was an empty jewel case on him, from the Oldham shop."

"That's right, sir," said Rymer. "But we couldn't get him to talk …"

"Wait," said McKendrick. "He did manage to get out a couple of words before he passed out … 'Grey Moose'."

"The same words exactly!" said Falconer, his eyes lighting up. "But what the devil do they mean? It might be a brand of pressed beef –"

"Or one of these American cigarettes," put in Rymer. McKendrick waved aside these interruptions. "It must mean something," he insisted. "Two dying men don't speak the same words exactly just by coincidence."

Falconer nodded slowly. "I see what you're driving at, sir," he said. "You think these two were in on those jobs, and the gang wiped 'em out so as to take no chances of their giving the game away. They sound a pretty callous lot of devils."

"I should say that it's the head of this organisation who's behind these – er – liquidations," mused Sir Richard. "They're quite obviously part and parcel of his plans."

"Then you agree with Falconer that there is an organisation?" queried Rymer abruptly.

Sir Richard rubbed his forehead rather wearily with his left hand while he continued to turn over reports with his right. At last he closed the folder. "That seems to be the only conclusion, Inspector," he said with a sigh. "If they were just the usual small-time safe-busters, like Peter Scales, or Mo Turner, or Larry the Canner, the odds are we'd have got one or more of them by now. They'd try to get rid of the stuff through one of the fences we've got tabs on, and we'd be on to them. But the head of this crowd has obviously got his own special means of disposal."

"That's true," agreed Falconer. "We haven't traced a single item in all those jobs yet."

"He could be holding on to the stuff till it cools downs," Rymer suggested.

"I shouldn't imagine that's very likely," said the Assistant Commissioner, thoughtfully tracing a design on his blotting pad with his paper-knife. "I can't help agreeing with Falconer that we're up against something really big, and we've got to pull every shot out of the locker. Now, are you absolutely sure there was nothing about the Gloucester job that might give us something to go on?"

He looked from one to the other and there was silence for a few seconds. Then Falconer slowly took a bulging wallet from his inside pocket and extracted a piece of pasteboard about half the size of a postcard. "There was this card," he said in a doubtful tone.

Sir Richard took the card and examined it carefully. "Where did you find it?" he asked.

"In the waste-paper basket just by the safe of the Gloucester jewellers'. As you see, it was torn into five pieces, but it wasn't difficult to put it together."

Sir Richard picked up a magnifying glass and placed the card under it. On the card was printed in imitation copperplate handwriting:

WITH THE COMPLIMENTS OF HARRY DENVER.

"So that joker from America has popped up again," murmured Sir Richard. "Where's the catch this time?"

During the past year or so Scotland Yard had come to know this strange young man from America, with the mobile features, rimless glasses, and ingenuous smile, rather too well; the presence of Harry Denver usually meant trouble for somebody. As often as not it was for some unscrupulous operator, either inside or on the verge of the underworld, but the police were usually none too pleased about it because the matter invariably entailed a long and complicated prosecution, even when Mr Denver had prevented them with indisputable evidence. And what particularly annoyed the police was the fact that Harry Denver always emerged as debonair and unruffled as ever, and often several thousand dollars to the good. The Yard chiefs had experienced a pronounced sensation of relief when Harry had bought a small Manor House not far from Sevenoaks and proposed to devote his energies to collecting pewter and playing the country Squire.

"Where's the catch?" repeated Sir Richard, turning the card over and peering at it again.

"In the first place," replied Falconer, "Harry says he's never set foot in Gloucester in his life."

"Well, you know what a confounded liar the fellow is," retorted McKendrick. "Have you checked on him at all?"

"The jewellers say they've never set eyes on him," said Falconer.

"I don't suppose they've set eyes on any of the gang that did the job," observed the Assistant Commissioner sourly. "Did you find out if he had an alibi?"

"Yes, he had an alibi all right. He was up in Town for the night to see a girl named Sue Raymond in a new musical – seems he knew her in New York. He stayed the night at the St Regis – got in soon after midnight. According to the doctor, the night watchman had been chloroformed about that time – and the Constable found him soon after 2 a.m. So Denver simply couldn't have been in Gloucester then."

"You never can tell with that customer!" said Rymer sceptically.

"I questioned the night porter at the St Regis – he knows Denver well and swears he never left the place while he was on duty," Falconer assured him. He turned to his chief again. "There's another thing about that card, sir."

"Eh? What's that?"

"There are no fingerprints on it. I used rubber gloves when I put it together, and whoever tore it up and put it in the

7

waste-paper basket must have done the same. Now, if Mr Denver left that card deliberately why should he go to the trouble of using gloves?"

"He might have been wearing them anyhow," Rymer pointed out.

Falconer shrugged. "Yet again, if he wanted to leave a card, why tear it up?"

Sir Richard rested his chin on his hand and nodded thoughtfully. "Yes, I can see what you're driving at," he murmured. "You think this card business is a plant – presumably to distract attention from the real master mind."

"That's about it, sir," agreed Falconer. "Denver's name has been in the papers several times – and there was that silly article about him being the modern Robin Hood. It's given somebody an idea."

Sir Richard picked up a wire paper-fastener and very deliberately clipped the card to the report of the Gloucester robbery. "You haven't seen Denver?" he asked.

"No, sir. I spoke to him twice on the telephone. He seemed a bit surprised at first, then rather amused. But he helped me all he could about the alibi when he saw how serious it was."

"Alibi or not, I think we should keep an eye on that gentleman," Rymer suggested.

"That sounds like a good idea," replied McKendrick. "You know him fairly well, don't you, Falconer?"

"I certainly saw something of him in the Blandford case."

"All right, then you can pop down to his place and have a talk to him as soon as you can get away from here today. And if you get the slightest hint that he is the brains behind this gang, don't take any chances. Just tell him you're rechecking his alibi."

"It isn't easy to fool Harry Denver," said Falconer, slipping his little black notebook into his pocket.

"I must say, sir, I'm not convinced that it is a real organisation we're up against," insisted Rymer. "What makes you so sure about that?"

Sir Richard began to pace up and down between his desk and the fireplace. "It's more a hunch than anything," he confessed. "For one thing, they've tackled such a variety of jobs – the average safe-buster sticks to one line as a rule, and goes after the sort of stuff he can get rid of without much trouble. This delignate gang have already robbed a cinema, a bank, two jewellers, and a factory office. It takes a very unusual brain to plan such a variety of jobs in a comparatively short time."

"A brain like Harry Denver's?" queried Rymer.

Sir Richard McKendrick did not reply.

CHAPTER TWO

Caldicott Manor was a sturdy four-square white house standing about half a mile outside the village of Caldicott Green, near the junction of the main road to Sevenoaks some four miles away.

From the moment he set eyes on it in an agent's catalogue the Manor had intrigued Harry Denver, who had been suddenly overcome with the idea of retiring into the heart of the English countryside and getting back to nature after his exciting and profitable incursions into the London underworld.

He also liked the look of Caldicott Green, with its small stream running parallel to the main street and draining into a large pool near the Manor which offered possibilities for fishing, one of his favourite forms of relaxation. Mr Denver was burdened with overlarge and slightly troublesome feet which debarred him from most forms of sport. Angling, however, was ideal, for it allowed him to relax at full length for long periods on sunny afternoons, taking the weight off his pedal extremities. Harry claimed that many of his best ideas had come to him while sitting beside a placid stream, hopefully awaiting a bite which never materialised.

His enemies declared that Harry suffered with his feet because he was too big for his boots, and there may have been something in this accusation, for this young man from America could have bluffed his way into the secret councils of the Atomic Control Commission as nonchalantly as if he were the man who originally split the atom. But the secret of his success lay in the fact that he never over-estimated himself; his bluffs were always a part of a coolly calculated scheme and designed for a specific purpose.

Naturally, having enriched himself to some considerable extent at the expense of a wide variety of social parasites, he had made a number of bitter enemies, so he was not in the least surprised to hear of the attempt to implicate him in the jewel robbery at Gloucester. It was by no means the first time such a thing had happened; in fact, he was surprised that it had not occurred more often.

Harry Denver lay on the enormous settee in his drawing room (that was what the previous tenant had called it) awaiting the arrival of his nearest neighbours, Dr Grant and his niece, Sally Harrison, with whom he had scraped acquaintance at a nearby point-to-point meeting. They had promptly invited him to lunch, and he was now about to return their hospitality. Harry had not planned to intermingle the local country folk, but he had to admit that the doctor and his niece rather intrigued him. The niece in particular.

Sally, who bore not the slightest resemblance in features to her uncle, seemed right out of place in the heart of the Kent countryside. Harry had met plenty of her type in the night spots of New York; in fact, she awakened vague murmurings of nostalgia inside him. Blonde, brittle, perfectly made-up, exquisitely manicured, Sally looked as if she had been born with a lipstick in one hand and a drink in the other. She had a lively turn of conversation which amused Harry. She was a cynic to the tips of her blood-red fingernails and he liked meeting people who had no respect for those who sat in the seats of the mighty. But he found it hard to believe that she was Dr Grant's niece and thought it idly intriguing to speculate upon their exact relationship.

Grant was a man in his early fifties, a very energetic type, somewhat wizened by many tropical suns. He had told Harry that he had worked on the Gold Coast for some years before his retirement, and he certainly talked knowledgeably about certain parts of the world so that he made a most agreeable dining companion. But there was a slight air of mystery about him. He ran a couple of large cars and horses for himself and

Sally, and to all outward appearances seemed to live at the rate of about ten thousand pounds a year.

Harry was pondering on these and other minor matters while he smoked one of his favourite Chesterfields, when the telephone rang and his butler, Miles, came in to tell him he was wanted.

Harry had always had a yearning for the genuine type of old English butler he had seen in so many indifferent British films. He had interviewed over thirty applicants for the job, and Miles came nearest to the genuine article. This was possibly because Miles had played such a part in no fewer than sixty-eight films, and was now driven to play it in earnest as a result of the parlous condition of the British film industry!

Although Miles had carefully omitted to mention to his employer that his experience had been confined to the sound stages at Shepperton and Pinewood and had not extended to the stately homes of England, Harry was fortunately not over-fussy about details of domestic routine and was completely satisfied so long as his butler looked the part. He delighted in watching Miles throw open a door and announce in nicely modulated tones – as he was doing at this moment – "There is a Superintendent Falconer who would like to speak to you on the telephone, sir."

Harry gave Miles an appreciative grin, then slowly placed his slippered feet on the floor. "Okay, Miles, I'll take it."

Superintendent Falconer wanted to know if he might drop in a little later that evening, and Harry assured the detective that he would be delighted to see him. He was just replacing the receiver when the front door bell rang and Miles opened the door to usher in his guests.

Apologising for his slippers, Harry led them into a tiny conservatory which he had converted into a cocktail bar, and commented on the fact that Sally was looking particularly attractive.

"I adore you Americans," she laughed. "You always say exactly the right thing at the right moment. Now I feel that the three hours I spent at the hairdresser's wasn't entirely wasted."

Harry grinned. "If only I'd known, I'd have invited some more people," he assured her. "You're worth a much bigger audience!"

She accepted a cocktail and sipped it appreciatively, but Dr Grant preferred whisky and drank three before dinner, explaining somewhat apologetically that it was the sundowner habit he had developed in the tropics. This was the doctor's cue for a series of stories about his adventures which lasted half-way through dinner, despite cynical comments from Sally.

Miles served the meal impeccably and poured coffee from the silver coffee-pot with such dignity that, as Harry whispered to Sally, you expected to see a curtain go up at any minute and find yourself starting on Act Two.

The doctor went on drinking whisky, which appeared to evoke longer and more lurid reminiscences, until at last Harry turned to Sally and inquired pleasantly, "What about your past, Miss Harrison? Haven't you ever had any hair-raising adventures?"

"I dare say," she replied noncommittally, "but I guess I know when to keep my mouth shut." She looked across at her uncle meaningly, and he seemed to take the hint for soon afterwards he announced that they must be going. It was after nine-thirty and there was still no sign of Superintendent Falconer, for which Harry was secretly thankful; he was not particularly anxious for his country neighbours to suspect that he had any dealings with the police as he was well aware how rumour can distort and magnify in the rural areas.

Still discoursing upon the origins of sleeping sickness, the doctor banished into the night, holding his niece's arm rather more tightly than would have appeared necessary. Ten minutes later Miles announced Superintendent Falconer with the quiet aplomb of the trusted retainer who is acquainted with every skeleton in the family cupboard.

Harry had seen Falconer quite frequently when they were concerned with the mysterious dope smuggling that had been centred upon the police station in the little Thames-side town of Blandford. Harry had eventually traced it, by what he modestly termed a stroke of luck, to the police Sergeant of the station, who had been using his Lost Property Department as a distribution centre.

Starting by disliking each other to some extent, Harry and the Superintendent had been mildly surprised to discover that they had mutual interests, such as fishing and American cigarettes, and a weakness for unorthodox methods. Falconer had risen to his present rank by reason of his alert mind that showed a genius for by-passing routine procedure and getting quick results.

Harry favoured the same methods, but was the first to admit that it was much easier for him to apply them, for he did not have to contend with a massive list of rules and regulations. Since their first meeting they had occasionally enjoyed a drink together at the hostelry just round the corner from New Scotland Yard, comparing notes about their mutual acquaintances in the underworld and elsewhere. They were slightly startled to discover how many times they had reached exactly the same conclusions.

Harry waved Falconer to the most comfortable armchair and asked if he had had any food.

"Thanks, Harry, I snatched a quick supper on the way down – that's why I'm a bit late," said the Superintendent.

"Well, at least you'll let me give you a drink – Miles, a whisky for Mr Falconer."

Miles took the drink over to Falconer, then crossed to Harry and murmured discreetly, "I'm sorry, sir, but we are almost out of whisky. The doctor was – ahem – a trifle heavy on our last bottle."

"Good Lord!" exclaimed Harry. "Is it as bad as that? I must nip down and see George Bates at the Kingfisher." He turned to Falconer. "Perhaps you'd like to run down to the local with me? The landlord there lets me have the odd bottle of my favourite brand now and them. We can have a quick one while we're there – it's not a bad old pub, and there's a stuffed pike in the 'snug' that will interest you …"

Falconer smiled and nodded. Miles withdrew and closed the door silently behind him.

Harry carefully placed his feet on his favourite fireside stool and grinned at the Superintendent. "Well, Falconer, is somebody still trying to put the smear on me?"

Falconer took a gulp at his whisky and leaned back in his chair. "It's still the same smear," he replied. "The chief isn't altogether happy about your alibi."

"Well, that's just too bad," murmured Harry, rubbing his chin with his long, sensitive fingers. He reached for a packet of Chesterfields and flicked one over to Falconer. "You tell your boss he's darn lucky to find me with such a good alibi. It isn't once in a blue moon I stay the night in Town; I wouldn't have done this time if I hadn't taken my girlfriend on to a night spot."

"She could corroborate all that, I suppose, if necessary?"

Harry frowned. "Say, what's going on now?"

"You didn't take her home, I suppose?"

"I put her into a taxi in Piccadilly just on midnight – we'd have stayed on later but she'd had a hectic day and wanted

15

some sleep. Then I went straight back to the hotel, just as I told you. You don't think I'm pulling a fast one, do you?

"No, no, of course not, Harry," said Falconer with a worried expression. "But these gelignite robberies have got us all a bit rattled. Close on one hundred thousand pounds' worth in a few months."

Harry pursed his lips thoughtfully.

"Chee, somebody's thinking big for once in a while," he commented. "Looks like they're trying to nationalise the crime racket."

"So you see, Harry, the A.C, is out to follow up every clue like grim death. He's convinced – and so am I, for that matter – that this is a large organisation under the direction of a master mind. And if we can take a short cut to the master mind the sooner we'll clear up the business."

Harry blew out a large cloud of smoke. "Are you trying to tell me that your boss suspects that I'm the big black chief?"

"He wants to make absolutely certain that you're not," said Falconer earnestly. "After all, he knows you're pretty cute, and you've been around quite a bit on both sides of the Atlantic. You're the sort of unknown quantity that might well be in charge of a gang of this sort – not that I think for a moment –" he added hastily.

"I appreciate that!" grinned Harry.

"But you see," went on Falconer, "he's got to eliminate as many possibilities as he can. Also, he thought you might be able to give him some inkling as to who would be likely to want to plant the Gloucester job on you."

Harry shrugged. "It might be any of the boys and girls – Princess Vaniscourt, Skeff Larabie, Billy Sorrell; they'd murder their own mother if they thought they could frame me."

Falconer took another gulp of whisky and looked round the room for a minute without speaking. Then he said somewhat cautiously, "This is a very nice place you've got here. You've done nicely for yourself, Harry."

Harry grinned again. "Meaning where did I get the doh-ray-me? Do we have to go into all that? Maybe you'd like to see a signed statement from my accountants?"

"No, no, of course not." Falconer looked distinctly uncomfortable. "I'm sorry, Harry, but we're all a bit nervy about this business. There hasn't been anything this big for some years now, and I dare say one or two of us will be out of a job by the time it's over." He leaned forward in his chair and looked directly at his host. "Are you quite sure you haven't any ideas about it, Harry?"

Harry Denver flicked the ash from the end of his cigarette. "To tell you the honest truth, old man, I've hardly given it a thought. I've been concentrating on rusticating these past few months."

Falconer took out his wallet and passed over the visiting card with the copperplate inscription. "Can't you think whose work that's likely to be?" he inquired seriously.

Harry flicked the card with his fingernail. "Your guess is as good as mine," he said.

"You've never had any cards like that yourself?"

Harry shook his head. "I've never bothered about visiting cards – always thought they were kinda old-fashioned."

"You haven't sent anyone a present with a card like that enclosed?"

"No; in any case I'd use my own handwriting." He paused for a moment, then asked, "If you've come here to collect my fingerprints to see if they tally with those on the card, go right ahead, brother!"

Falconer gloomily shook his head, and took another drink. "There aren't any smudges on the card; at least, there weren't when I found it," he said. "That's what made me suspicious.

If you'd wanted to advertise the job as your work you wouldn't have taken the trouble to bother about fingerprints."

"Nor would I have bothered to tear up that card," ruminated Harry. "And if I had really wanted to get rid of the card I wouldn't have been such a mug as to leave it lying around in a trash-basket."

"It might have led us on a pretty involved false trail if you hadn't happened to have that alibi," said the Superintendent. "I'd have had to set a couple of men on to tail you night and day."

Harry laughed and passed the card back to Falconer, who replaced it in his wallet.

"This gelignite gang interests me," said Harry Denver, wriggling his toes inside his slippers. "I always like meeting people with new ideas. Tell me more about the set-up, that's if it isn't top secret."

Falconer filled in the details of the chain of robberies very rapidly, but there was little that was new to Harry, who had read most of the accounts in the newspapers. When Falconer had finished, Harry poured the remainder of the whisky into his guest's glass.

"About this night watchman at Gloucester," he murmured. "Did you see him before he passed out?"

"Yes," said Falconer. "He was an old lag named Hiller, and he'd had a heavy dose of chloroform; too much for his heart."

"Then he didn't say anything?"

"Well, he did come round just before the end, and he whispered two words quite distinctly – 'Grey Moose'. For a minute I thought perhaps he might be talking nonsense, then I remembered."

"What did you remember?"

"Just after the gang pulled the Oldham job we picked up a man named Smoky Pearce, run over by a lorry on the Preston road. Just before he died he said the same two words."

"Grey Moose," repeated Harry thoughtfully. "It might mean anything … some sort of password maybe …"

"It doesn't suggest anything to you?" queried Falconer, eyeing him closely.

"Not a thing – except that I seem to have seen the words somewhere – can't call it to mind right now. It might be some sort of trade name."

"We've been into all that," nodded Falconer. "But you'll agree that when two dying men say the same thing it must have some sort of significance, especially as they were both suspected of being linked with the gelignite gang."

"You got something there," agreed Harry thoughtfully. "I wish I could help you, brother, but I guess I've had enough of the crime racket to last me for a while. All I want to do is mooch around, a little fishing, a trip to Town once in a while, a lot of relaxing, and a drink at the local … and that reminds me; we'd better get going if we don't want to be shut out."

He fumbled for his shoes and put them on with a certain amount of effort.

"How far is this pub?" asked Falconer.

"It won't take us five minutes in the car," Harry told him. "I think you'll like the Kingfisher – it's a fairly old inn – oak beams and all that – dates back quite a way. We Americans are always suckers for tradition."

"You're also suckers for Scotch whisky," said Falconer with a faint smile as they went out.

Harry's car was an enormous American roadster, but the engine seemed to be cold and missed on two of its cylinders all the way to the inn.

"I guess the plugs are getting clogged up," frowned Harry as they drew up in front of the Kingfisher Inn. "I'd better run her round to the back and take a quick look at 'em. It won't take a minute. You go in and order the drinks – be sure to tell Bates they're on me."

Falconer got out and Harry ran the car into the small car park at the back of the inn, where he manoeuvred it until the bonnet was exactly under the solitary electric light. Then he took out the offending plugs and carefully cleaned and replaced them. He was a little longer than he had anticipated because an elusive blob of grease on one of the plus was made than usually obstinate.

He had replaced the bonnet and was just about to switch off all the lights when there was a shout from inside the Kingfisher. Then a door opened and there was the sound of running feet. Harry immediately recognised the short, stubby figure of George Bates, the landlord of the inn.

"I thought it was your car, Mr Denver," he gasped breathlessly.

"Anything wrong, George?" asked Harry, noting his obvious distress.

"Was that feller with you – the bloke what just come in?"

"Yes, of course. Didn't he tell you to put the drinks down to me?"

"That's right – but I was a bit suspicious like, as I'd never seen him before. And then, while my back was turned, it happened … My God, it's awful!"

"What's happened?"

"Why he … shot himself!"

The little innkeeper's eyes seemed to bulge right out of his head, and he clutched at the mascot on the front of Denver's car as if he were about to faint.

CHAPTER THREE

Harry Denver reached inside the car and took out a silver flask from one of the side pockets. He unscrewed the top and passed it to George Bates. "Drink this," he ordered.

The innkeeper took the flask in a shaking hand, gulped down a mouthful of brandy, and passed it back. Harry slipped it into his pocket ready for further emergencies.

"All right, Mr Denver," the landlord said hoarsely. "We'd better go in now and see if there's anything we can do."

"Okay then, come on! No time to be lost!"

They went in through the back door, along a short passage, and into the saloon bar.

"I've locked the front door, sir," breathed Bates's hoarse voice behind him as Harry went into the room. He stood for a moment on the threshold as if to establish a clear impression of his surroundings.

The body of Superintendent Falconer was almost the first thing he saw, for his attention was directed to it by an overturned table and stool in a far corner of the saloon. The body lay nearby, with a trickle of blood flowing from the head and a revolver clasped in the left hand.

On Harry's left was the service room which was connected to the saloon by an enclosed counter and opened out into the bar usually patronised by local farmworkers. Apparently the house had been empty of customers at the time of the suicide and there was no one about now. Harry was not altogether surprised by this, for George Bates was constantly grumbling about the lack of custom although the brewery had spent a considerable sum upon refurnishing the saloon with small tables, imitation antique settles, and stools.

Harry went across to Falconer, placed a finger on the neck artery, then turned to Bates. "Anyone else around?" he asked.

"I told the Missus to stay in the kitchen. And there's Mr Dancey upstairs …"

Harry took in the room – the little service counter with its row of bottles on shelves, the new chromium-plated beer engine, the cash register, advertisements for cigarettes and soft drinks, the heavy china ashtrays, and the solitary siphon at one end of the counter …

George Bates shifted uncomfortably from one foot to the other. "Can't think what made 'im do it, Mr Denver," he burst forth at last. "Never known such a thing in all me born days, 'e comes in here and orders two double whiskies and the moment I turn my back –"

"Can I use your telephone?" asked Harry somewhat abruptly.

Bates nodded in the direction of the passage, where Harry found the instrument in an alcove. He was connected to the police station and spoke to the Sergeant in charge. The police surgeon was not available so Harry suggested that the Sergeant should get Dr Grant as he was comparatively near at hand.

Bates was still standing nervously in the doorway of the saloon bar when Harry returned. He had obviously overheard the conversation.

"What did you mean, Mr Denver, when you said it <u>might</u> be suicide?" Bates demanded with an aggressive note in his voice.

Harry ignored him and went over to the body of Falconer, stooped to examine the revolver for a moment, then turned again to Bates. "What were you doing when this man came in?" he asked.

"A crossword," was the prompt reply. "The place was as quiet as the grave – I 'ave to do something or I'd go barmy."

"You were standing behind the bar?" asked Harry.

"That's right. He come in and ordered the whiskies – said they was to be charged up to you – and just as I was going to pour 'em he asked me if I could change a pound note. So I went off into the sitting room to get the money, and when I get back he's lyin' there just like he is now, with that gun in 'is 'and. It give me a real turn – thought for a minute I was goin' to pass out. Then I hollered to the Missus to stop where she was, and come out to see if you were 'ere like 'e said."

"How long were you out there?" asked Harry, nodding in the direction of the sitting room.

"About three or four minutes, I dare say. I 'ad a bit of an argument with the Missus about 'arf a dollar she'd borrowed from the petty cash."

Harry thrust his hands deep into his trouser pockets and sat down on one of the stools. "I suppose someone could have come in here while you were in the sitting room?" he suggested.

Bates rubbed the back of his head with his rather grubby hand. "I reckon they might," he conceded. "They could 'ave come from upstairs or through the front door."

"What about that door over there?" Harry indicated a door to the right of the bar.

"That's the club room, only used one night a week by club members. I always keep it locked, on account of the stuff in there."

"What sort of stuff?"

"Oh, you know – robes and chains of office, and all that tomfoolery."

Harry walked over to the door and tried the knob. It was locked. He paced back to the bar, picked up one of the two empty glasses which were standing side by side, and poured out a generous measure of brandy from his flask. He glanced inquiringly at the landlord, who shook his head.

"No more for me, Mr Denver."

Harry sipped the brandy thoughtfully. A solitary car went past outside. They could hear the clock ticking in the public bar.

Suddenly George Bates said, "Funny I never heard that gun go off. Nor the Missus neither or she'd soon 'ave –"

"Not much mystery about that," replied Harry absently. "If you look at the gun you'll see it's fitted with a silencer – that cylindrical gadget fastened to the end of the barrel. There'd only be a sort of quiet pop."

"Cor, 'e didn't 'arf make a job of it, and no mistake!" ejaculated the innkeeper. "But it beats me what he wants to come 'ere for. Never set eyes on 'im in me life before."

"You're quite sure about that?" said Harry quietly.

"Course I'm sure. Who is 'e, anyway?"

"Oh, just a friend of mine. By the way, did you say there was someone upstairs?"

"That's right. An old gent, name of Dancey. Bit of a queer bird, if you ask me. Got 'ere yesterday afternoon. Says 'e's on a tour of the county. Asked me all sorts of questions about this place. There wasn't much I could tell 'im, I've only been 'ere six months myself."

"I think you'd better ask Mr Dancey to come down here," decided Harry.

George Bates seemed surprised. "What do we want the old geezer nosing about for?" he asked.

"The police Sergeant will be sure to want to see him when he gets here, so we might as well break it to him gently."

George Bates shrugged. "Okay with me if you say so, Mr Denver!"

Harry watched him go out, muttering, and make his way towards the stairs in the passage. He had always felt a vague dislike for this little man but had tried to be friendly, as he had been with most of the folk round about. But there always seemed to be something lacking about the atmosphere at the

Kingfisher Inn; there was none of that warm bonhomie one associated with the typical British country pub. Which was, no doubt, the reason why most of the locals patronised the other inn in the centre of the village.

When he heard the landlord's footsteps reach the top of the stairs Harry crossed swiftly to the till and cautiously rang up "No Sale". He examined the contents of the drawer, then closed it carefully and stood, apparently lost in thought, until he heard distant voices from the stair-head.

However, Bates returned alone and said that Mr Dancey would be down in a minute.

"I broke it to 'im," he went on, "and he took it as if I was passing the time of day! Never turned a blinking 'air! If you ask me, he's a tough one, that Mr Dancey!"

Harry lit a cigarette and wondered how much longer the police would be. For the first time the full implications of Falconer's death impressed themselves upon him. The Superintendent had come to see him about his possible connection with the gelignite gang; Harry had brought him down here for a drink and he had either committed suicide or had been murdered. Scotland Yard were likely to become very difficult from now on, and it looked as if he would be involved with this case whether he liked it or not.

A sound outside the door cut short his reflections and he swung round to see Mr Dancey standing in the doorway.

Dancey was a lean, white-haired man with a small beard, and wore a neat dark blue suit, and curiously enough, a fancy waistcoat. Harry judged him to be in his late seventies. Dancey took one look at the body, then turned away.

After introducing himself Harry led the old man to the settle where he sat facing away from the body. "As the dead man was a friend of mine, Mr Dancey, I thought perhaps you wouldn't mind answering a few questions, just for my private information. Of course, the police will probably ask you much the same questions, so it may help you to get things straight in your mind."

"I'll be only too pleased," replied Dancey with a little smile, "but I'm afraid I can't help very much. What is it you want to know?"

"Well, now," said Harry, "I wonder if you could remember what time it was when you went to your room tonight?"

Mr Dancey hesitated for a moment, then said, "It was just before ten o'clock. I sat reading for a short while. I happened to come across a most interesting book about this part of the world and –"

"Quite so," put in Harry suavely, hoping to head the old boy off what was obviously a favourite theme.

"This affair must be quite a shock for you, Mr Denver," he went on. "The idea of a friend committing suicide is very distressing, an act of sheer desperation that is beyond the comprehension of many of us –"

"Mr Dancey," Harry interrupted again, "what makes you so certain that this is suicide?"

For a moment he seemed a trifle bewildered. "What makes me so certain?" he repeated in a puzzled tone. "What else can it be, Mr Denver? Unless, of course, Mr Bates shot your friend."

There was a faint clatter from behind the bar as George Bates dropped a glass, which he had been wiping, back into the washing-up water.

"'Ere, what are you getting' at?" His voice sounded unduly harsh, and the back of his neck turned a deep red. He came from behind the bar, still clutching the towel. He drew himself up to the full extent of his five feet two inches and glowered down at Mr Dancey. "What should I want to kill 'im for? Never set eyes on 'im in me life!"

Mr Dancey stood up and peered at the body. "There doesn't seem to be very much blood, Mr Bates," he announced a trifle wistfully.

"There's enough to give me the willies," retorted George Bates in a grating tone. "This isn't no laughing matter, I can tell you. Blokes 'ave lost their licence over affairs like this before today." A thought seemed to strike him and he swung round and confronted Dancey. "If it comes to that, you might 'ave done it yourself! You wasn't in bed when I knocked at your door."

"That's quite true, Mr Bates," he said calmly. "I happened to be reading."

"Have you decided to stay here long?" interrupted Harry, conscious of the passing of the valuable minutes.

"I haven't quite made up my mind," replied Dancey. "Most probably till the end of the week."

This was the cue for George Bates to intervene once more. "You didn't say nothing about that when you signed the register," he reminded him. "You said it was only for the two nights."

But Mr Dancey was in no was dismayed. He treated George Bates rather like a recalcitrant child. "It was my original intention to remain here only two nights, but I found this part of the world so extremely interesting."

"You don't say!" exclaimed the landlord with heavy sarcasm.

"Indeed I do. This inn must be at least five hundred years old – I refer to the outside walls, of course – and the beams! They are quite magnificent!"

"You can 'ave 'em," sniffed the landlord. "I been 'ere six months too long for my likin'."

"I'm sure it all seems quite snug," said Dancey politely. "I should have thought you would get quite a number of tourists …"

George Bates did not deign to reply. He looked across at the body once again and shivered. "Them police are a long time gettin' 'ere," he muttered. "Wish they'd hurry up … it fair gives me the creeps to see 'im lying' there, starin' at nothin'." He turned to Denver. "Couldn't we cover 'im up, sir? Just till the police come … it wouldn't do no harm."

"Good idea," agreed Harry.

"All right. I'll get an old sheet from the linen cupboard," nodded Bates, as he hurried out of the room with some alacrity, obviously relieved to get away from the sight of the corpse. He went off upstairs, and they could hear him opening a cupboard.

Dancey sat quite still for a minute or so without speaking. Then he slowly walked round the room, pausing for some seconds to peer again at the body. Presently, he said, "Was he a very great friend of yours, Mr Denver?"

Harry shrugged. "I hadn't known him more than a year or so. But he was a good guy. We got along."

Dancey nodded. "I thought for a moment his face was familiar, but I see now that he's quite a stranger to me."

"His name was Falconer. He was a Superintendent at Scotland Yard."

Mr Dancey was suitably impressed. "Scotland Yard?" he repeated. "Dear, dear, that makes it even more serious, doesn't it?"

"It certainly is very serious," agreed Harry.

Dancey walked over to the door which led into the club room and bent down to examine the floor. "Is it my imagination, Mr Denver, or is there a damp patch here by the door?"

Harry went over to him. "M'm, it could be," he agreed. "Perhaps somebody spilt their beer."

"There's hardly been anyone in all evening," Dancey told him. "This – er – moisture is quite recent – as if someone had cleaned up a mess of some sort."

"You mean," said Harry quietly, "it could be blood?"

"I'm not saying so," replied Dancey hastily, "but it must be <u>something</u>."

Harry measured the distance from the body with his eye. It was quite ten feet … and if the blood came from the body why should anyone wish to clear it up before the police arrived? Harry shifted his weight from one foot to the other and stared pensively at the locked door.

When George Bates returned with the sheet and covered the body, Harry said quite casually, "Have you got the key to that club room handy?"

A shifty look came into the landlord's eyes. "I'm not supposed to let anybody in there," he replied defensively.

"Somebody goes in to clean the place?" queried Harry softly.

"Of course they do – the Missus does it. But it's a private room. What d'you want to go in there for?"

"Mr Dancey and I thought we'd like to take a look around."

George Bates was obviously reluctant to comply with Harry's request. "There's nothing to see in there, I tell you – just a table and some chairs …"

"In that case," said Harry, "there can be no possible harm in our taking a look." He hesitated a moment, then said meaningly, "The police will almost certainly want to see in there."

"I don't see why they should."

"It's fairly obvious, I'd have thought," said Harry. "A murderer might have left some trace."

"Murderer!" gasped Bates. "Mr Denver, you don't really think –"

"I think you'd better give me that key," replied Harry smoothly.

Mumbling to himself, the landlord went over to the till, opened the drawer as far as it would go, and took out the key. Then he joined Harry and Dancey at the door of the club room.

The key fitted easily; he opened the door and switched on the light …

As he had said, it was just a bare room so far as furniture was concerned, apart from a small table and about a dozen chairs. Opposite the door a large cupboard occupied almost half the length of the wall.

Harry nodded in its direction. "What's in there?"

"Oh, their robes and chains of office, and all that sort of rubbish," sniffed Bates. "Like a lot of kids they are, playing dressing up."

The room smelt strongly of disinfectant Harry noticed as he made for the cupboard. As the landlord had said, it was full of shapeless robes and decorations. Meanwhile, Dancey was stooping to examine the floor.

Harry closed the cupboard door and joined Dancey. "When did you say this room was last used?" he asked George Bates.

"Why, on club night – last Thursday," the landlord replied.

"Then how do you account for this damp patch on the floor?"

Bates was on the defensive again. "There's always damp comin' through the floors in this place," he snarled. "I can't 'elp that, can I?"

Harry looked round for an ally in Dancey, but found the old man studying an insignia mounted above the fireplace. "Founded in 1756," he was murmuring to himself. "How very interesting … Mr Denver, have you seen this? It's a sort of coat of arms …"

Harry strode to the fireplace and read the inscription under his breath.

"Loyal Antediluvian Order of Bison … Grey Moose Lodge 1478 … Grey Moose …"

CHAPTER FOUR

Harry looked round cautiously, somewhat apprehensive that his low whisper might have been overheard. But Dancey gave no hint of having noticed anything unusual, and George Bates was moving over towards the door as if to hurry them out.

"I must remember to make a note to look into these ancient orders," Dancey was saying. "I'm sure one could write a whole book about them. I'm quite certain it has never been done before." He turned to the landlord. "Can you tell me who runs this – er – lodge?" he asked.

George Bates sniffed. "Yes, it's a feller named Dimthorpe – keeps the greengrocers in the village. And you won't get much out of <u>him</u>," he added in a surly tone.

While Dancey gossiped to the landlord Harry peered at the shield above the fireplace, with its second-rate reproduction of a moose's head and somewhat faded gilt lettering. Of course, it might be just a coincidence that the gelignite gang had some connection with a Grey Moose Lodge – there must be scores of others in various parts of the country. But he could not help feeling that Superintendent Falconer's death had some connection with this room. Maybe he had been inside himself and seen someone; George Bates could have been lying about the place always being locked. He suddenly realised that Dancey was talking to him.

"May I ask if you have any information about the history of these ancient orders?" he was asking.

Harry came back to earth with a start. "Me, sir? Why, not very much, I guess. I went to one or two Elks' dinners when I was in the States, but I can't say I ever really belonged."

"What exactly is the purpose behind these organisations?"

Harry shook his head. "You have me there, brother! I had some good times with the Elks, but I don't remember anyone performing any good deeds."

32

A fleeting expression of annoyance flitted across Dancey's features, but he obviously had no intention of abandoning the idea. "There must be some source where one can obtain such information," he mused. "After all, secret societies are against the law … at least, I think they are … Or would that be one of those Defence Regulations?"

Harry broke open a new packet of Chesterfields and offered Dancey one. The old man refused, and Harry lit one for himself. He didn't know what to make of this old boy, but he was hardly a sinister type. All the same, the strangest people got mixed up in murder, folks who looked as if the sight of the merest scratch would send them into a dead faint.

Harry was suddenly conscious of a car approaching in the distance. Its engine came nearer, roared for a few seconds, then stopped. Two doors opened and slammed, and there were footsteps outside. George Bates hurried off to open the front door, and Harry and Mr Dancey returned to the saloon, closing the club room door behind them.

Almost at once they heard voices, the suave tones of Dr Grant mingling with the richer, country dialects of Sergeant Hubble and the Constable with him. It seemed that the doctor had picked them up in his car and there had been a slight delay in locating the Constable. Harry knew them both by sight but had never done more than pass the time of day with them.

While Dr Grant examined the body the Sergeant questioned George Bates, the Constable slowly taking down his replies in longhand. The Sergeant had already been acquainted with the dead man's identity and fairly bristled with self-importance. Year after year he had patiently awaited the call to Scotland Yard, the big assignment, the congratulatory pat on the shoulder from the Commissioner. Now his probation was over. Scotland Yard had come to him!

Sergeant Hubble was out to show his superiors just how a job like this should be handled; all the evidence very much to the point, nothing overlooked, and no nonsense from any of the witnesses! This case was going to be run exactly as Sergeant Hubble wanted it.

While the Constable took down one or two minor details from George Bates the Sergeant strolled across to where Dr Grant was kneeling beside the body.

"Ah, revolver in the left hand," noted Hubble at a quick glance, making a mental note of the fact. The doctor pulled away the sheet and began his examination, first asking for as much light as possible. George Bates went out into the passage and pressed down two more switches. Having made certain that there were no other visible signs of violence upon the body Grant turned his attention to the head wound which was undoubtedly the cause of death.

Sergeant Hubble began to take a few notes on his own account, concerning the position of the body in relation to the rest of the furniture, a description of the Luger clasped in the dead man's left hand, and the exact position of the wound in the head.

Apparently he did not leap to the conclusion that Falconer had committed suicide, for he sent his Constable to make a thorough investigation of the other rooms for trace of a possible intruder.

Meanwhile Harry Denver and Dancey sat patiently at the far corner or the bar, awaiting their turn to be questioned. For some reason best known to himself the Sergeant had apparently decided to defer this until the doctor had completed his examination. From time to time Dancey went on prattling, half to himself, about the history of friendly societies, craftsmen's guilds, and similar institutions, while Harry puffed moodily at his cigarette and said very little.

At length Dr Grant replaced his instruments in his worn attaché case and rose somewhat painfully to his feet. "The man has been dead for just over half an hour, I should say," he announced. "He must have died almost instantaneously. The bullet penetrated the brain." He turned to the Sergeant. "Would you like me to make a full written report?"

"If you'd be so good," nodded Hubble. "The police surgeon won't be back for a few days. It was lucky you were available, or I'd have had to telephone Sevenoaks."

The doctor signalled to George Bates and asked for a strong whisky, which was very quickly poured out. With a keen sense of his responsibilities the Sergeant refused a drink. However, Harry accepted one, and while he was sipping it the Sergeant came over to him.

"I understand that the deceased was a friend of yours, Mr Denver," he began respectfully.

"Not exactly a friend," returned Harry with equal politeness. Let's say a close acquaintance. He'd come down to see me on a matter of business."

The Sergeant's bushy eyebrows were raised at that. "You mean Scotland Yard business, Mr Denver?"

"That is so."

Hubble bit his pencil, hesitating how to frame his next question. "Could that business have had any connection with this unfortunate affair?" he asked, with a certain deliberation.

"It could have," replied Harry, his tone remaining as noncommittal as before. "That is, if this turns out to be a case of murder."

"Then you don't think it might be suicide?" persisted Hubble somewhat portentously.

Harry shook his head. "The Superintendent seemed like the last man in the world to commit suicide."

"You don't happen to know if he's been suffering from ill health?"

"Not to my knowledge. They'll tell you more about that at the Yard, I dare say."

The Sergeant paused to make several notes and Harry sipped his whisky. Dancey sat with an air of polite attention, as if he were listening to a lecture.

"Did you come here for any particular reason tonight?" continued the Sergeant.

"The usual reason," answered Harry with a faint grin. "I'd run out of whisky at home, and we wanted a nightcap before closing time. I stayed to clean up the plugs in my car and the Superintendent came in ahead of me to order the drinks. Mr Bates here has told you the rest."

"All this happened about ten o'clock, I take it?"

"Yes," nodded Harry. "Round about ten o'clock, I should say."

The Sergeant jotted down some further notes, then turned to George Bates. "I'd like you to go over your statement again, Mr Bates, he said pleasantly. "Just to make sure that nothing has been left out and so that the doctor can hear it."

With a certain reluctance George Bates agreed. "I was standing behind the bar doing me crossword puzzle when this fellow come in and ordered a couple of whiskies and says put 'em down to Mr Denver. Then 'e asks me if I can change 'im a quid, so I goes off into the sitting room to get the money. When I come back I see him lyin' there, just like 'e is now."

"You're quite sure there was no one else in any of these rooms?"

"Only my Missus in the back, and Mr Dancey upstairs. I never saw anyone else."

"And you heard nothing?"

"Not a sound – there's a silencer thing on that gun," added the landlord confidentially. "They only make a noise like a kid's pop-gun."

"How do you know that?" snapped the Sergeant.

"I watch the telly when I get the chance!" retorted the landlord with a certain acerbity.

"All right, there's no need to be funny," growled Hubble. "We've had enough trouble here as it is, without you putting in any back answers. Don't forget you're the most important witness, and I warn you that you'll have to keep your wits about you."

"I've told you the truth and that's all there is to it," replied George Bates obstinately. "You know as much about it as I do now."

The Sergeant looked round the room. "Is this gentleman staying here?" he inquired.

"Yes, Sergeant," said Harry. "This is Mr Dancey."

For the first time the Sergeant became really conscious of the keen brown eyes of the gentleman in question. He crossed over to Dancey and stood with his arms akimbo. "Well, sir, can you help us to throw a little light on this affair?"

"I'm afraid not, Sergeant," replied Dancey, meeting his gaze quite confidently. "This sort of thing is rather outside my province, you know. In fact, I can't recall ever having set eyes on a dead man before in my life."

"Where were you when this happened?" interposed the Sergeant, to forestall any possible reminiscences.

"In my room, reading. Mr Bates came up to tell me what had occurred, and naturally I was extremely upset."

George Bates sniffed. "You didn't look very upset to me."

Dancey turned to him with an injured air. "One does not always display one's emotions to strangers," he said quietly. "You may remember my saying that I would follow you downstairs in a few minutes. I needed a little time to collect myself."

There was something slightly pathetic about Dancey's dignified restraint, and Harry found himself feeling rather sorry for the old boy. At the same time he had to admit that

Dancey appeared comparatively unruffled and dispassionate about the tragedy that had just occurred. Harry imagined that he might be a retired schoolmaster, for he was treating the Sergeant's inquiries with the same patience one would display towards an over-persistent pupil. Nevertheless, the Sergeant found him a far more agreeable witness than the landlord, for he made cool and accurate replies to his questions with no hint of blustering or concealment.

"How long have you been staying here, Mr Dancey?" he inquired.

"I arrived yesterday afternoon – I am making a short tour of these parts."

"Could I have your full name and permanent address?" he asked.

"Benjamin Dancey, 17 Quadrant Row, Bayswater, London," he announced, and the Sergeant wrote it down very solemnly.

"You may be needed as a witness at the Inquest, Mr Dancey. I'll let you know about that later when I've had a word with the Inspector."

"Have you any idea when that will be?"

"Probably tomorrow afternoon."

At that moment the Constable returned to report that he had discovered nothing unusual in any other room in the house, and that he had made a thorough search of any possible hiding places both inside and outside.

The Sergeant was frankly puzzled. He was very doubtful whether an exalted official of Scotland Yard would commit suicide in a small country inn: on the other hand, nobody seemed to have seen any murderer. He went over to Harry and checked that he had seen no one leave from the back of the inn while he had been in the car park. And the landlord had seen no one else enter or leave through the front. All the same, he was not entirely satisfied about George Bates, and presently he tackled him again.

"Now, Mr Bates, I want to get this little matter cleared up. Think carefully – could anyone have come in here while you were in the back room getting that change?"

Bates rubbed the back of his hand. "Yes," he decided. "They could 'ave come in 'ere either from upstairs or the street."

"What about the back door?"

"I reckon I'd 'ave 'eard anyone who came in that way. The door sticks and makes a jarrin' sort of noise when you open it."

"And you didn't hear anyone come downstairs?"

"I didn't 'ear anyone," replied Bates, "though I'm not saying anyone mightn't 'ave crept down very quiet like." He looked meaningly in the direction of Dancey, who was, however, gazing thoughtfully into the fire, apparently quite unconscious of any insinuation.

Somewhat baffled, the Sergeant instructed his colleague to telephone for an ambulance to take the body to the mortuary, then recollected himself and abruptly cancelled the order. The Inspector would probably want to see everything exactly as it was. He was inclined to be fussy and unwilling to accept a report from an inferior officer, no matter how detailed or reliable it might be. Besides, he might even decide to call in Scotland Yard.

Sergeant Hubble, somewhat lamely, ordered the Constable to telephone Inspector Martin at Sevenoaks. It would have been nice to be able to present the Inspector with an open and shut case, but things very rarely worked out that way in real life; only in those cheap paperback thrillers his fourteen-year-old son was always reading. Anyhow, there wasn't much more he could do, for he was certain that if this was a case of murder the person responsible was no longer on the premises.

There might be some sort of clue in the way of fingerprints, but they were going to take a bit of sorting out in a public room of that sort which was used by all and sundry for eight hours a day. The "smudges" on the gun itself would almost certainly prove to be those of the dead man.

The Constable returned to say that Inspector Martin would be at the station in twenty minutes and would the Sergeant meet him there.

"I'll run you back if you like, Sergeant," volunteered Harry, and the Sergeant gratefully accepted the offer.

Harry went off to start his car, saying he would pick the Sergeant up outside the front door. Hubble gave instructions to the Constable, who was to remain in charge during his absence, then turned to thank Dr Grant for his help.

The doctor cut short Hubble's apologies for troubling him. "I'm only too glad to have been able to give a hand, Sergeant. It reminded me of old times on the Gold Coast. I remember once when I –"

But the appearance of Denver cut short his reminiscences, and as he was going the Sergeant turned to speak to Dancey. "It will be all right for you to go back to your room, sir," he said respectfully. "I doubt if the Inspector will want to see you tonight."

Dancey permitted himself a circumspect little smile. "Thank you, Sergeant, and you too, Mr Denver," he murmured gratefully and wished everyone good night.

Harry smiled politely and watched him until he was out of sight. Quite frankly, Dancey puzzled him. He hardly looked a sinister type, but you could never tell with these odd eccentric little characters.

Harry and the Sergeant made a move towards the door but George Bates called after them. "What am I supposed to do about that?" He indicated the body. "We can't just leave 'im 'ere all night."

The Sergeant waved aside the interruption. "I'll attend to that presently. Pearman will look after things here till I get back." He turned to the Constable and ordered him to keep a close watch on the front door. "Don't let anyone in."

"You want me to wait and see the Inspector?" queried Dr Grant.

"If you wouldn't mind, Doctor. Just a formality."

"I'll be delighted." The doctor looked as if he meant it, for he had settled down in the most comfortable chair with another glass of whisky.

Outside, the engine of Harry's saloon roared for a moment, doors slammed, gears changed, and the sound of the car slowly receded into the night.

What seemed to be an oppressive silence fell upon the house. The Constable went over to the body, pulled the sheet further over the head, and perched on a stool.

A minute or two went by, then George Bates suddenly said, "Why don't we go into the back room? There's still a good fire – looks more cheerful."

"Good idea!" approved the doctor, getting to his feet.

"What about you, Mr Pearman?" asked the Landlord.

The policeman shook his head. "I think I'd better stop in here, if you don't mind."

"Please yourself. We'll be out there if you want us."

George Bates and the doctor went out along the short passage to the little back sitting room where a small but lively fire was burning between the two old-fashioned hobs. The doctor set his glass, still half full, on the table, and made himself comfortable in a well-worn rocking chair, while George Bates closed the door with some care.

"Where's your wife?" asked the doctor as soon as he was settled.

41

George Bates made an upward gesture with a grimy thumb. "Packed 'er off to bed out of the way," he answered.

They began to talk in low voices.

"I don't like this business, Doc," said George Bates in a hoarse, apprehensive voice. "I ain't never been mixed up with anything like this before." His Cockney origin became more apparent than ever in his agitation.

"Don't be a damned fool!" snapped Grant in low tones. "Everything's turned out all right. You've only got to keep your wits about you." His face was redder than usual, possibly because of the quantity of whisky he had drunk that evening.

George Bates leaned against the mantelpiece and looked in to the fire. "It's tricky, Doc. I can't think what the devil brought 'im 'ere – of all places. D'you think he'd found out anything?"

"Well, nobody'll know the answer to that now," replied Grant grimly.

"It's a nasty business," repeated Bates. "I don't like the looks of that Mr Denver. 'E's a queer bird, if you ask me."

"Yes," nodded the doctor. "I've read one or two things about him in the papers; we'll have to keep an eye on him."

"What's 'e want to come and live in these parts for?" demanded Bates curiously.

"He's very fond of fishing."

"That's what he says. But I don't trust 'im, I've got a feeling 'e's up to something."

"Pull yourself together," said Grant, taking a gulp at his whisky. "It's quite simple. Falconer came down to see him because of that card left behind on the Gloucester job."

"Card? What card? I don't know anything about –"

"Skip it, and give me another drink. You don't have to worry about Harry Denver. We'll look after him."

The landlord opened a cupboard, took out a bottle, and filled two glasses. "I thought for a minute 'e'd got wise about the club room – 'e asked to go inside – and found a damp patch on the floor where I put up the –"

"You damn fool! What did you want to let him go in for!" The doctor was on his feet now, towering above the little innkeeper.

"I 'ad to let 'im in. 'E said the police would want to go and 'ave a look round … It'd 'ave looked fishy if I'd tried to keep 'im out."

The doctor sat down again. "He never mentioned anything about the club room," he reflected. "Maybe he didn't attach any importance to whatever he saw there."

"Anyhow, 'e can't prove nothing," nodded the innkeeper. "I'm the only witness, and I got my story."

"Of course you have," rallied the doctor. "There'll be no trouble."

For a minute or two they drank in silence.

Then Bates said suddenly, "'Eard anything about the next job?"

"Yes," nodded the doctor. "Brighton."

"Ah …" George Bates nodded several times. "Plenty of stuff down there if you know where to lay 'ands on it."

"It's practically settled," Grant told him. "We'll be meeting on Thursday."

"Not 'ere?" exclaimed the landlord in some alarm.

"Why not? This business will be all over by then. It'll be as safe as anywhere." The doctor drained his glass for the ninth time that evening. "This is a big job at Brighton," he went on. "One of the biggest we've taken on yet, and we've got to leave nothing to chance."

He got up and went over to the door, opened it a few inches, and closed it again before adding quietly, "I had the tip this morning that Grey Moose may be coming down here himself."

CHAPTER FIVE

"How ever did I get on without you, Miles?" demanded Harry Denver lazily, levering himself into a slightly more comfortable position in his armchair.

His butler smiled politely without offering any reply.

It was just after nine on the Thursday morning after the death of Superintendent Falconer, on whom the Coroner had returned an open verdict. There had been plenty of sensational headlines during the past few days, but the police did not seem to be much nearer establishing the exact cause of their colleague's death. Crime reporters with varying degrees of imagination speculated upon the case from a number of angles, and two or three played up Harry Denver's connection with it. They would not readily forget the young American's comparatively recent exploits amongst the strange characters in and around the London underworld, and as it was known that Falconer had been investigating the gelignite robberies the natural inference was that Harry Denver was in some way linked up with that gang. This resulted in a number of brisk young men, usually wearing shabby raincoats, being seen in the vicinity of Caldicott Manor during the past two days. Most of them had called at the house but had been duly repulsed by the faithful Miles who, having performed just such an operation some forty times in a wide assortment of film productions, was able to command a variety of techniques suitable for any emergency.

Harry gazed out of his French windows across a vista of Kent orchards while Miles methodically read reports from all the morning newspapers of the Inquest on Superintendent Falconer. His own evidence was detailed quite fully but gave no clue as to the reason the Superintendent had visited him on that fatal evening. As he had caught sight of Inspector Bowen from the Yard in close consultation with the Coroner just before the Inquest, Harry guessed that this omission had been carefully arranged.

All the reports of the Inquest so far had proved reasonably discreet until Miles turned to the melodramatic pages of the *Daily Reflector* with its lively display of two-inch headlines and bathing beauties on each alternate sheet.

"This is a little more sensational, sir," began Miles with a slight apologetic cough, deferentially inclining his head exactly as he had done in some long since epic. He started to read a report with the byline *By Our Crime Correspondent*.

"Playboy Harry Denver was a guest of New Scotland Yard chiefs last night, when he discussed with Chief-Inspector Rymer the incidents leading to the tragic death of Superintendent Falconer at the Kingfisher Inn, near Sevenoaks, which was the subject of yesterday's Inquest. Further sensational disclosures may be expected in the near future."

Harry wriggled his toes inside his very comfortable slippers and asked Miles to pour him some more coffee.

As the butler passed the cup to Harry he said quietly, "I forgot to tell you, sir, that a gentleman called to see you when you were in London yesterday."

"Really?" said Harry with some interest. "Did he leave his name?"

"Yes, sir. It was a Mr Dancey."

"Dancey?" repeated Harry thoughtfully. "Now I wonder what he wanted."

"He didn't say, sir. He seemed quite a pleasant gentleman, but he wouldn't leave any message. He said he might call again if you didn't get in touch with him. He's staying at the Kingfisher."

Harry nodded absently and deftly extracted a cigarette from the silver box on the small table beside him. As he lit it Miles asked, "Shall I go on reading the reports, sir?"

"No, that'll do for now, Miles. You'd better run along and see cook about lunch – or whatever you do at this time of the morning."

The butler hesitated. "I'm afraid several of those reporters are likely to call again this morning, sir. You won't be making any statement to the Press?"

Harry unlatched the French window and opened it to admit the cool morning breeze. "No, Miles, I guess we won't be making any statements just yet awhile. As far as the Press boys are concerned I've always found it pays to say as little as possible."

Miles nodded approvingly. He rather enjoyed rebuffing the gentlemen of the Press.

Harry perched on the top stone step, which was already quite warm from the early morning sunshine, and gazed out across the orchards. A tractor was chugging away busily somewhere nearby, and there was something vaguely reassuring about the neatly shaven lawns and trim, well-kept borders.

"This is the life, Miles," Harry murmured. "Folks are crazy to stifle themselves in towns … what is it some poet fellow says about a flask of wine, a loaf of bread and thou …?"

"Yes, sir, that reminds me," said Miles, who was still hovering near the window. "One of the reporters who called yesterday was a young lady – a most attractive young lady."

Harry wagged an indolent finger. "Now, Miles, take it easy."

"She was most insistent, sir. In fact, she refused to take 'No' for an answer."

"That's too bad," murmured Harry. "Blonde or brunette?"

"I beg your pardon, sir?"

"I said was she dark or fair?"

"A sort of chestnut I think would describe her colouring, sir."

"Very nice, too. Did she leave a name?"

"Yes, sir. She was a Miss Diana Stone."

"Diana Stone," Harry repeated thoughtfully. "I've seen that name some place. He searched amongst the pile of newspapers and found a copy of the *Daily Messenger*, and folding back the pages he turned to a column headed *Feminine Fancies*. There, at the foot of the column, was the name he sought.

Harry chuckled. "I've been in some queer places in my time, Miles, but I've never been in a heart-throb column before! I guess it's all experience, as the chorus girl said when she stepped into the crinoline."

"Quite so, sir. And if Miss Stone calls again am I to tell her –"

He was interrupted by the peal of the front door bell.

"That's probably Inspector Rymer," said Harry as Miles went off to open the door. "Better show him in here."

Harry wandered back to the French windows. The morning sunshine was very tempting. He stretched himself, yawning mightily, and was about to step out onto the terrace when his attention was caught by the sound of raised voices inside the house. Miles seemed to be expostulating with a girl who was displaying some signs of persistence.

"I'm sorry, madam," he heard the butler say, "but Mr Denver is expecting someone else." Harry could not catch the girl's reply but Miles went on, "I'll ask Mr Denver, but he's very busy …"

The door opened and Miles came into the room and crossed to where Harry was standing by the window. "It's the young lady I mentioned just now, sir," he said quietly. "Shall I tell her to wait until after the Inspector has gone?"

Harry frowned thoughtfully for a moment, then said quickly, "No, I'll see what it is she wants right now. All right, Miles, let her in."

A voice from the doorway called out, "Don't bother – I'm in already."

For some seconds Harry stood and appraised her from her trim chestnut curls down to her slim nylon clad ankles. "Well, well," he murmured at last, "I guess you're one of those girls who knows her way around."

She smiled as if she really meant it and moved forward a couple of paces with an elegance he could not fail to note. "I'm sorry," she said frankly, "but it really is terribly important."

"If you're going to tell me the old one about being flung out on to the hard pavements of Fleet Street unless you go back with a story, skip it!" advised Harry. "I used that one myself when I was a cub reporter first year out of college."

"You've given up reporting?" she asked.

"I guess I was flung out one day when I didn't go back with a story," he admitted with a rueful grin. "But you'd better sit down now you've come all this way." He dismissed Miles with a casual nod and indicated an armchair for the benefit of his visitor. He opened the silver cigarette box and indicated the English and American brands in their separate sections. He was slightly surprised when she chose the American.

"Well, he's certainly a throwback to the good old days," she smiled, indicating the departing butler.

Harry snapped his lighter and held the flame to her cigarette. "Yes, he kinda makes me feel good," he told her with an understanding nod. "Worth every cent I pay him."

She settled back in her armchair and puffed out a stream of smoke very deliberately. Harry admired the dark green dress she was wearing beneath her coat. Not a day over twenty-five, he told himself; a girl who'd be exciting to take around or come home to. He found himself trying to get a glimpse of her left hand, and experienced a slight feeling of relief to note there was no ring on the slim, well-manicured fingers.

"You'll be Miss Diana Stone?" he inquired politely as he lit another cigarette for himself.

She nodded.

"Well, this is an honour," went on Harry in a suave tone. "Will you be wanting to write a piece about this fine old English manor with its Tudor chimneys and –"

She shook her head decisively. "No, Mr Denver, I've come to see you about something much more serious than that. I shouldn't be here at all really, I should be at the office. I'm very conscientious about my job, so you can guess I wouldn't come running down here without a very good reason."

"Then your visit has nothing to do with the *Daily Messenger*?"

"Not a thing. I'm afraid I rather misled your butler – I used the paper's name because I was so anxious to see you. I'm sorry if it upset you in any way."

"Think nothing of it," said Harry with a lazy gesture. "There's nothing I like better than being kept out of the *Daily Messenger*!"

She threw her head back against the chair and laughed. It was an infectious little laugh. But she became serious again almost immediately.

"Well, I'm rather busy this morning," Harry told her. "I had some thought of going fishing. I suppose that's a bit outside your sort of column, Miss Stone, though I shall be glad to show you –"

"Mr Denver," she interrupted in an earnest manner, "do you think Superintendent Falconer committed suicide?"

Harry paused in the act of flicking the ash from the end of his cigarette. "Really, Miss Stone, that's what your English lawyers call a leading question, isn't it?"

But Diana Stone was not to be diverted. "I'm serious about this, Mr Denver."

He suddenly realised that there were tears in the grey eyes. Even so, he wasn't particularly impressed. Harry had met far too many women who switched on the tears as easily as they powdered their shapely noses. He recalled particularly a pretty little confidence trickster who "worked" the transatlantic luxury liners with just such a display of ready emotions and had relieved many a dollar millionaire of a nice little bunch of travellers' cheques.

For all Harry knew, the very personable young lady who sat opposite might be a tool of the gelignite gang sent to pry into his affairs or plant some new evidence against him. For all he knew, she wasn't even Diana Stone. She might simply have picked on that name and called herself a newspaper woman …

The girl seemed to guess what was passing through his mind, for she suddenly opened her bag, fumbled in it for a moment, and passed him a neat red card.

In some perplexity he looked at it. The card testified that Miss Diana Stone of the *Daily Messenger* was a paid-up member of the National Union of Journalists, and requested that she should be afforded full facilities available to members of the Press.

Still looking somewhat bewildered Harry passed back the card. "I don't get it," he said. "Have you turned crime reporter, or what?"

Once again she fumbled in her handbag and this time produced a postcard photograph. "I have a very strong personal interest in this case," she said. "Now, will you look at this … and then take another look at me."

He recognised the photograph at once; it was one of Superintendent Falconer, taken some fifteen years ago, he estimated. Falconer wore an open-necked shirt and a sun helmet, and the buildings in the background looked rather like a South African farmhouse. Harry glanced across at the girl. The resemblance was obvious.

"David Falconer was my brother," she said simply. "Now do you believe me?"

With a sigh Harry returned the photograph. "I believe you," he said slowly.

"Then will you answer my question? Did he really commit suicide?"

Harry hesitated. At last he said, "Just between ourselves, I'm not at all satisfied about your brother's death. When he came to see me he was certainly very worried about this gelignite gang but he certainly wasn't in the desperate sort of mood one associates with suicide."

"Then it *was* murder!" she exclaimed emotionally. "I knew they'd get him, I knew it!" Her hands trembled in nervous excitement as they fingered the clasp of her handbag. She was leaning forward and trying hard to fight back her tears. "I always warned David … but he never took me seriously …"

Harry went to the sideboard and took out a decanter of Napoleon brandy, from which he carefully poured about a dessertspoonful into a liqueur glass.

"Drink this first, then we'll talk," he said briefly.

She took several sips and the colour which had drained from her face began to surge back again. Then she set the glass on a small table nearby and said quietly, "I need your help, Mr Denver, more than anything I've ever needed in my life before."

Harry slowly sat down and propped his feet on a footstool. "Then your real name is Falconer?" he queried.

"That's right. Everybody knows me as Diana Stone – it's part of the paper's publicity stunt to boost the column. I'm not supposed to give away my real identity."

"It's a very nice name … Diana Stone," Harry remarked, saying it slowly. "All right now, tell me what you meant when you said you knew they'd get your brother."

She hesitated. "Well, it's rather a long story. Will you answer me one question first?"

He nodded encouragingly and she went on, "What did my brother come to see you about the night he died?"

Harry blew out a ring of smoke and watched it rise. "I shouldn't tell you this," he said, "but your brother had reason to believe I might be implicated in one of these gelignite gang jobs. He came down to ask me one or two questions. Unfortunately for the gang, I had rather a good alibi for the night the affair occurred."

"And he didn't mention any of his theories about this gelignite gang?"

"We didn't get very much time. I rushed him off to the Kingfisher for an extra bottle of whisky, and I thought we'd probably have a good talk when we got back."

"You don't know anything about my brother's earlier experiences abroad, then?" she asked.

"Not very much. He wasn't a particularly talkative character; you know that as well as I do." He wondered vaguely when she would come to the point.

"Almost eight years ago," she began, "David was attached to a special branch of the Cape Town Constabulary. They were very busy at the time with a series of daring raids – mostly on jewellers and diamond warehouses. My brother and another officer were in charge of the investigation and it was very tough going. After several months they discovered who was the leader of the organisation. It was a man who went by the name of Carl Kranston."

52

"I seem to remember reading about that affair," nodded Harry. "Go on."

"This man Kranston was a very shrewd customer; well educated and widely travelled. He knew the underworld in half a dozen countries and he stopped at nothing. But the police pulled in several members of the gang and one of them told all he knew, so they found out quite a lot about Carl Kranston. But Kranston had provided for that emergency and when the police made a big round-up of the gang he managed to escape."

"That's right," put in Harry. "I seem to recall hearing about him being in Chicago the following year."

"Not long after he fooled the police," continued the girl, "the officer who'd been working with my brother on the case was murdered. It wasn't a very pleasant murder. Almost immediately after that there were two attempts on my brother's life."

Harry whistled softly. There was a strained look in her eyes as she recalled those distressing days with an obvious reluctance. "I suppose there was no evidence against Kranston?" he queried.

"Not a trace. The police officer's body was found by a farmer in a roadside ditch. He'd been terribly beaten up by someone who had apparently kidnapped him and dumped him out in the country."

"Looks to me as if this Kranston guy's got a nasty kink in his imagination somewhere," mused Harry. "What about the attacks on your brother?"

"They might have been accidents. I don't think he was taking any chances with David because the police were very much on his tail by that time. He tried to get David just outside Cape Town one day. A large saloon car swerved and David only just leapt clear in time. He couldn't see the driver, and there was no back number-plate. The other time, David

53

was walking along one of the main streets when a big wooden crate, weighing about a ton, crashed down on the pavement a few feet away. They swore the rope had slipped, and David couldn't prove otherwise, but I can still remember how suspicious he was about the whole business. He was terrified that Kranston would find out he had a sister. I was living with relatives then, and he made me adopt an assumed name. When things were very tense he wouldn't even telephone me in case the line was tapped. He knew Kranston would stop at nothing. There was something quite devilish about the man; it was as if he rejoiced in evil for its own sake as well as for the money it brought him."

Harry leaned over and flicked the ash from his cigarette. There was no mistaking this girl's sincerity, but he had a feeling that she might be a little overwrought, which was quite natural, of course, in view of her brother's sudden death. "You said Carl Kranston got clear from the country just in time?" he murmured.

"Yes. But David had a letter from him soon after, saying that Kranston would get even one day, and ever since he's received threatening letters at regular intervals. The last was just before this gelignite gang started its activities, and right from the moment David was put on the case he's had a feeling he was up against Carl Kranston. He warned me weeks ago that I must lie low and use the name Diana Stone everywhere."

It was Harry's turn to look worried. "What made him think it was Carl Kranston?" he demanded.

"I don't quite know. Just a sort of hunch he had. Maybe he found something similar between the way the gang worked and the old set-up in Cape Town. David's hunches in that line were usually pretty reliable and he grew more and more certain as time went on. It was he who finally convinced the

Scotland Yard chiefs that they really were up against a big organisation."

Harry reached out and rang a bell at the side of the fireplace, and when Miles promptly appeared he asked him to bring some coffee.

As the butler closed the door silently behind him Harry said, "I could kick myself for letting your brother out of my sight that evening. I had a feeling he was going to spill something …" He sighed. "Well, I guess we all make mistakes and pay for 'em. The question is – where do we go from here?"

"Then you do believe me? You believe I'm telling you the truth?" There was a note of relief in her voice.

"I believe you, ma'am," replied Harry evenly. "But I don't know if that helps very much. We've got no proof that Kranston is behind this gang, or that he killed your brother. We don't even know what he looks like. I suppose your brother never met him?"

She shook her head. "That's just the awful part about it. Carl Kranston has always escaped the police records in every country he's visited. Some other poor devil has always taken the rap for his crimes, and the international police haven't even as much as a photograph." There was a trace of bitterness in her voice. "David used to tell me that Kranston built up a completely new identity for himself in every country. Sometimes he'd spend more than a year doing it before he planned a new coup."

"Looks like this guy knows the answers before he hears the questions," mused Harry. "All the same, I wish I knew why he picked on me over that Gloucester job. I've never done him any harm … At least, none that I know of."

"But don't you see," she urged, "he probably thinks you're a friend of David's. He may have seen you two together – suspected you were working against him, and decided to get in the first blow."

Harry stubbed out his cigarette with a decisive gesture. "Young lady, this business is getting a darn sight too complicated for my liking!" he pronounced. "I'm a peace-loving guy. – Oh, I'll admit I've had my hectic moments with the crooks and the cops, but right now all I want to do is relaxin' and fishin'. I've kinda got used to this pleasant country routine; it's in my blood now. I don't go for the big-time skulduggery any more." He paused with a faraway look in his eyes and added, "Why, if I could happen across a real nice girl I might even think of getting hitched up ..."

She flung her cigarette end into the fireplace and leaned forward impulsively. "Mr Denver, you know as well as I do that David was murdered, and you've got to help me!"

He sighed again. There was something very pleasant about the large grey eyes, the quivering lips …

At that moment Miles came in with a large pot of coffee, a silver jug of milk, and a plate of Harry's favourite biscuits.

Diana Stone's expression was noticeably less strained now and she drank her coffee with obvious enjoyment, complimenting her host on its quality. When he had refilled her cup he suddenly returned to the subject they had been discussing.

"Do you happen to know if your brother had any sort of a dossier on Carl Kranston?" he inquired.

She shook her heard a little dubiously. "Not to my knowledge. Of course, he knew an awful lot about him but he'd never put it on paper, so far as I know. The day before he died he seemed to have some sort of presentiment. He telephoned me at the office and asked me to meet him on the bridge in St James's Park. We sat on a seat, and he told me all he knew about Carl Kranston."

Harry jerked his feet off his footstool and sat bolt upright. "This is pretty serious," he exclaimed, "or it would be if Carl Kranston knew about it! It puts you in a very awkward spot – you realise that?"

"That's exactly why I came to see you. David told me to come to you in case of any trouble."

Harry looked doubtful. "You know, honey, I've a feeling I should pass you on to the police and tell them you need protection."

"I can look after myself," she insisted sturdily. "I'm not planning to run into danger unnecessarily. At the same time, I won't rest until the person who killed David pays for it."

"Looks to me like you're heading for trouble," observed Harry with a worried look.

But Diana appeared comparatively cheerful now that she was assured of his cooperation, for her brother had described Harry as "the dark horse that's always first past the post" and she had implicit faith in his judgement.

In fact, she seemed far happier about the present position than Harry was himself. He didn't really want to become involved with the gelignite gang and the prospect of having to keep a watchful eye on a comparatively helpless female wasn't nearly as inviting as the two or three months' fishing which he had planned. All the same, he was upset about Falconer's death and he would like to help the dead man's sister …

He toyed with the silver cigarette lighter and presently asked, "Did David know any special personal details about Carl Kranston? A birthmark, for instance?"

Almost at once she answered, "He has a small mark, caused apparently by a burn, just above the left elbow; and there's a girl named Sonya who frequently travels around with him." She paused for a moment, then added in a tone that was rather more tense, "And he never uses anything but a Luger."

Harry Denver clasped the arms of his chair. He could still see the figure of Superintendent Falconer stretched full length, with a dark stain of blood from the wound in his forehead, and his left hand clutching a dull black Luger revolver.

CHAPTER SIX

As Chief-Inspector Rymer did not arrive when expected Harry decided to stroll over to the Kingfisher Inn before dinner. He knew that Rymer had been busy there and hoped to find him still on the job.

Since the removal of the body of the unfortunate Superintendent the Kingfisher had become famous overnight. Motor cars, char-a-bancs, cyclists, and hikers arrived in multitudes, and George Bates had twice telephoned his brewery in Sevenoaks for fresh supplies of beer. Without any exception, the visitors betrayed a similar thirst for the gory details of the discovery of the body, and the landlord's voice had become quite husky as he retold the tale, even though he made frequent pauses for liquid refreshment.

Not many of the visitors paid much attention to the men in somewhat sombre raincoats who sat quietly in corners in the public rooms, taking stock of the visitors and comparing notes from time to time.

Rymer had drafted in these plain-clothes men, telling them it was unlikely they would be lucky enough to spot the murderer's return to the scene of his crime, but they were nevertheless to keep their eyes open just in case. After seeing them installed he went off in a police car, presumably to make further contact with the local police. When he returned several hours later they had nothing to report, apart from the shortage of beer, and Rymer went off again, saying that he would look in later.

It was during his absence that Harry Denver called in at the Kingfisher to find the saloon bar crammed with a very mixed collection of humanity. Having left a message with George Bates to the effect that he would be home all evening if the Inspector wanted to see him Harry strolled thoughtfully back to the Manor, pondering upon many things, including that strangely attractive young lady, Diana Stone. He was a little troubled as to what he was going to do about Miss Stone. Her work took her all over London and also into the provinces and he could not always be there to keep an eye on her.

Indeed, it seemed that Diana Stone was going to provide an unexpected complication in this affair. At first Harry had planned to keep out of it; now he did not see how he could. The only way to dispose of the danger was to put paid to the gelignite gang and its leader – supposing that leader to be Carl Kranston.

Harry had another important reason for wishing to steer clear of this case. He couldn't see what he stood to get out of it: hitherto he had consorted with criminals – and skated very near the edge of the law himself – only when he stood to gain substantially. He did not object to taking risks and exercising his ingenuity when he was well paid to do so, but he knew full well that the man on the side of the law rarely reaps any big returns. All the same, he could not forget Diana Stone …

***

Later that evening, when the Kingfisher Inn had relapsed into its usual state of desolation, the thick black curtains of the club room were drawn across the windows and the door was locked from the inside. Three men sat round the table examining a large-scale plan of the centre of Brighton.

Dr Grant, who seemed to be in charge of the proceedings, held a pencil in his right hand whilst he addressed himself mainly to two young men in flashy suits. George Bates hovered somewhat uncertainly in the background.

The room, which was lighted by a solitary bulb, smelt of stale tobacco smoke and disinfectant. Apparently the doctor was more than a trifle conscious of this, for he seemed to be pressing on with the business in hand as if there were no time to be wasted.

"Now, have you got it all clear, Joe?" he asked the round-faced young man in the flashy suit, whose hand held down one corner of the map. "We don't want any slip-ups on this job, or the Yard will be on us like a shot. How does the set-up look to you, Sam?" He turned to the taller of the two men, a swarthy individual with piercing black eyes and a thin, cruel mouth.

"I reckon it wouldn't do any harm to go over it again," Sam rasped, relighting the cigarette that hung from his lower lip.

With an impatient sigh the doctor returned to the map. "Sally will be parked here, just round the corner from West Street. All you have to do, Joe, is get the stuff out to her as fast as you can – hand it over, and then go back and mix with the crowd. Whatever you do, keep with the crowd until the police move them on. That's very important."

Joe nodded understandingly. "I looked the joint over this morning," he said casually. "Reckon I ought to be out in five or six minutes."

"Then that's all right," said Dr Grant. "Now, let's go over your piece, Sam. This is the first time we've done a daylight job, and the chief's a bit fussy about it all going off to schedule. In fact, it's got to look as if it wasn't our job at all. That's one of the main reasons for this new layout. It's all got to be spot on and through like clockwork, and then there'll be no come-back."

Sam Crawford signified his attention by the merest shrug of the shoulders. Since his National Service Sam had never been able to settle down to normal civilian life. He had, amongst other things, ridden a motor cycle in the familiar "Wall of Death" attraction with travelling fairs, then moved on to work for an organisation of stunt men who doubled for actors in film sequences which involved high risks to life and limb. But he grew tired of earning his money by law abiding

61

methods and linked up with one of the South London gangs, very soon acquiring a reputation for bringing off daredevil coups.

He placed a lean forefinger on the map. "That's where she parks the car?"

"That's correct, Sam. You see the jewellers' and the gown shop the moment you come charging round the bend – at three-forty on the dot! There'll be a good crowd in the street then. Now the chief is most particular that you shouldn't take any extra risks – we don't want a manslaughter rap pinned on to us. Got that?"

"Sure," he replied indifferently, as if this sort of job was really beneath his consideration. "Maybe I'll have to run some of the mugs down though. He wouldn't want me to let up just because some damn silly woman leaves a pram or something –"

"No, no," put in the doctor hastily. "You keep the horn going and they'll clear; then we want a real job made of that dress shop window. The glass is almost down to the ground so you shouldn't have much trouble. And as much noise as you like."

"Don't worry," growled Sam. "I'll wake up half the blasted town." He dropped his cigarette end on the floor and twisted his shoe over it. "I handed over the doings for the lorry last night, it's all fixed. We can have it any time, and enough juice to take us down there."

"Then that's all settled," said the doctor in a relieved tone.

"Thank Gawd I ain't driving that lorry," said George Bates.

Sam laughed. "It's a cakewalk," he sniffed.

"As long as it looks a genuine job the chief will be satisfied," said Grant.

"It'll be so genuine you can claim the insurance," Sam told him.

Joe fidgeted uneasily. "There's just one thing, Doc. Do I have to wait till I hear the smash before I get busy?"

Grant shook his head. "The chief says get going right away. You won't have any time to play with, but it shouldn't take any longer than the Gloucester job. Once you're inside you can work to the usual routine."

"I'll be out of the place in no time!" grinned Joe. "Have you got a list of the stuff?"

"I'm expecting Sally with it." The doctor glanced at his wristwatch. "She should be here any minute. The chief got the full list of stuff this morning …"

There was silence for a few seconds, then George Bates licked his lips and said rather nervously in a hoarse whisper, "You mean Grey Moose?"

The doctor inclined his head.

"Who is this bloke who calls himself Grey Moose?" persisted Sam. "He's been around for months now and we're no wiser. I reckon we got a right to know the feller we're working for. How do we know he won't double-cross us?"

Joe contradicted him with an expressive gesture. "I don't worry who the cove is," he announced. "He's cut me in over three thousand quid since I been in this racket, and when I get that sort of money I don't bother to ask questions."

"I'm not grumbling," nodded Sam, perching on the back of a chair. "I'm just sort of curious. You see, I'm used to knowing the bloke I work for. There's never been any harm in it yet." His tone had become slightly more aggressive and Dr Grant hastened to pacify him.

"Don't blame me, Sam – it's all part of the chief's idea. When we've made our last big clean-up he'll let us all in on everything. Up till then he doesn't want to take a chance on anybody recognising him at the wrong moment."

Sam muttered something under his breath; he was obviously by no means completely satisfied. But Joe

63

distracted his attention by asking further questions about the Brighton job.

"What happens after Sally gets away with the stuff?"

"She brings it back to my place here. Then I take care of it. It'll be in Amsterdam early next week."

"And when will the pay-out be?" inquired Sam.

"In about a week's time, I should imagine."

"Any idea how much the stuff will be worth?" asked Joe.

"I'm not sure," replied the doctor. "They carry a heavy stock at Dollands. We know there's a ring worth eight thousand pounds, and two sets of pearl earrings that run pretty high. I dare say Sally might know more about it. But the chief told me that they carry insurance for over sixty thousand pounds."

Joe whistled softly. "It's a blinking marvel how he finds out these things."

"Ah, he has his own ways of doing it," said Grant in a tone of mingled satisfaction and mysteriousness. "He's got sources of information that would startle Scotland Yard if they knew."

The doctor began to fold up the map very deliberately, and all the others lighted cigarettes. They were discussing the Brighton job in low tones when there came two distinct raps from behind the wall near the cupboard.

"That'll be Sally," nodded the doctor, and he went over to open the tall cupboard door. There was the sound of a sliding panel, and a moment later Sally stepped from behind a grey robe which concealed the secret panel. She was wearing a long evening cloak on which there were some traces of dust and cobwebs.

George Bates reached forward to close the panel but Sally stopped him. "Leave it," she said quietly. "The chief will be along in a few minutes."

The announcement caused something of a sensation. The men looked at each other with some uncertainty, then the doctor asked, "The chief's coming here?"

"Yes, I had a telephone message just before I left."

"But I thought he said –"

"He's changed his mind," interrupted Sally. "He's decided that this job is so important that he's got to talk it over with us himself. Also, he's got the money from the Gloucester job; it came through this morning."

"Blimey! That's quick work!" exclaimed Sam, who had now lost all trace of indifference. "I reckon there ought to be a nice packet for all of us …"

"There will be," promised the girl, placing several chairs in position around the table. She turned to George Bates. "Will you get a gin and vermouth for the chief? The same for me …"

The others murmured their orders and George Bates went off into the bar to fulfil them.

"The chief's taking a bit of a risk coming down 'ere so soon after that Falconer job," murmured Joe. "The village is full of plain-clothes men."

Sally smiled. "Don't you worry about the chief," she advised. "He can take care of all Scotland Yard if he puts his mind to it. But remember, everybody – if anybody talks about this job or squeaks about the chief he'll get 'em just as sure as he got the others."

George Bates returned with the drinks just in time to catch the sentence but nobody made any comment upon Sally's threat, except Joe.

"It's all right, Sally," Joe said reassuringly. "We know when we're well off. As long as Grey Moose plays it on the level with us we're sticking to him."

"You can rely on him," she insisted, opening the small evening bag she carried and taking out two sheets of mauve

65

notepaper. She passed the notepaper over to the doctor, who looked through them carefully then handed them on to Joe. "That's the Brighton stuff," he explained.

Joe took the paper and studied the typewritten list of valuables, each with a price against it. George Bates put down the tray of glasses and joined Sam, who was peering over Joe's shoulder.

"They must be mugs to keep all this stuff about the place," breathed the landlord, frowning at the list. "It must amount to thousands …"

"We've seen to it that they've got the stuff," Sally blandly informed him. "Just lately they've been getting a lot of inquiries which meant bringing down some of the best stuff in London."

"You see?" queried Grant with some satisfaction. "The chief takes care of everything."

Joe refolded the notepaper carefully and tucked it away in his inside coat pocket.

"This is going to be some job," he declared with a hoarse chuckle. He picked up his glass of beer and called out, "Here's to us and the Brighton job!"

The others had also taken their glasses and were about to drink when there was a sound outside the door.

"Who's that?" asked Sam in some alarm.

"It's all right," breathed George. "I locked it when I came in."

"If it's one of those damned detectives …" whispered Joe, taking a pace forward.

The doctor pushed him aside. "I'll handle this," he snapped, his hand going to his coat pocket.

But Sally interposed. "Don't be damned fools! Get out of sight through that panel. Leave this to George and me."

The door rattled.

"All right, George," nodded the girl. "Open up – and if it's a stranger tell him he's made a mistake …"

With some hesitation the landlord went to the door and turned the key. He opened the door about a foot and said in an uncertain voice, "I'm sorry, there must be some –"

But Sally's rippling laugh interrupted him. "It's all right, George. This is the chief!" She turned to the men inside the cupboard and called out, "It's all right, you can come out."

They came from their hiding place and saw the silent figure standing in the doorway.

"I thought you said the chief was –" began Sam, to be interrupted by Joe's exclamation of "This ain't the chief – it can't be Grey Moose!"

Dr Grant smiled. "I warned you fellows," he said. "I warned you."

CHAPTER SEVEN

On Saturday morning, at the end of an eventful week, Diana Stone sat in her plainly furnished office at Fleet Street House ruefully contemplating a pile of letters. She did not always come to the office on Saturday, for her secretary had the day off. But there had been a rush of correspondence during the past two or three days, following a question she had raised in her column, and she began to sort out the letters that could be easily answered, placing the others in a little pile to themselves.

She was busily making notes on the letters for the benefit of her secretary when her telephone rang and a familiar voice said, "Miss Stone – remember me?"

"Of course, Mr Denver! I was wondering if you'd phone."

"You're pretty busy, I guess?"

"Pretty busy."

"No time to help cement the ties of Anglo-American relations?"

"It rather depends what that involves." There was a flicker of amusement around her mobile mouth.

"I thought maybe we could have lunch some place," he suggested. "It'd do you good to get away from the grindstone."

She considered this for a moment, then said, "Where do you think?"

"If it's all the same to you," he replied after a moment's hesitation, "I'd like to make it Sevenoaks. I have special reasons for wanting to stick around these parts for a day or two, and there are some things I want to talk to you about. Can you make it?"

"I could be down there about one-thirty, if that suits you."

"That'll be fine. There's an hotel just along from the Post Office called the Star and Garter. You can't miss it. I'll be waiting in the lounge. Sure you can make it okay?"

"I'll be there," she promised, pushing the stack of letters into a folder with one hand as she replaced the receiver with the other.

Half an hour later Diana was following her own favourite course through the leafy roads of Dulwich. It was a sunny day, with a cool breeze stirring the treetops, and there were signs of activity on many of the sports fields she passed as the groundsmen made their preparations for the afternoon.

She reached the Star and Garter with just over five minutes to spare, and ran her car into the car park at the back of the hotel.

In the lounge Harry was talking to an elderly farmer whom he deserted as she came through the door.

"Right on time," he murmured approvingly. "I guess you're just about the first punctual woman I ever met. I was expecting to wait another half hour at the very least. We ought to have a drink to celebrate."

They sat in a corner of the lounge and sipped the drinks.

"What happened about those damp patches on the floor of the club room?" she was anxious to know. "You said you were going to mention them to Inspector Rymer."

Harry shook his head. "Afraid there was nothing much in that," he told her. "Rymer said he'd had the experts look at the patches but they couldn't find any traces of blood. If there had been any blood there someone had cleaned it up pretty thoroughly."

Diana sighed. "We seem to come up against a dead end whichever way we turn. But I still think that David was murdered."

He rose and took her empty glass. "Come in to lunch," he suggested. "We'll feel more like coping with life's little problems after a good meal."

They went into the long oak-panelled dining room with its low beams, glistening cutlery, and bleached table cloths. True, there was no deferential head waiter, but the young lady who deputised filled the breach very competently and brought them a meal that was obviously home-produced and cooked to perfection. The soup was innocent of any contact with tin; the chicken had not ranged its run for a day over ten months; the vegetables might have been picked from the garden an hour previously; and the tart was smothered with rich blackcurrant jam that had never been inside a factory.

Harry seemed determined not to discuss their present problem over lunch. He asked her a number of questions about her job, her experiences as a young reporter on a suburban paper in Cape Town; he discussed the shows that were on in London, with a passing reference to Sue Raymond which somehow made Diana feel vaguely uncomfortable. He even launched upon a long story of how he had persuaded a notorious woman confidence trickster to pay several thousand pounds for a practically worthless necklace who was under the impression that she would more than double the price of it.

"You seem to meet some very peculiar people," she observed as they sat drinking their coffee.

"Yes, I'm not what you'd call a highly respectable guy, I'm afraid," he sighed.

Diana laughed. "If you were highly respectable you'd probably be running a canning factory in Chicago."

"And then I'd never have had the pleasure of meeting you. I guess I like things the way they are."

They went on to talk about the differences between the American and English viewpoints, the film industry, the Arts

Council, the United Nations, the Beatles, and the immigration problem. Anything, in fact, but the activities of a certain Carl Kranston. Harry seemed strangely reluctant to discuss the sordid realities of crime with his guest, who in her turn appeared quite content to let the conversation drift pleasantly and await his leisure before turning to sterner topics.

After lunch, at his suggestion, they took a short stroll through the ancient main thoroughfare as far as the entrance to Knoll Park, pausing occasionally to peer into antique shops or examine an inscription on a tombstone in the churchyard.

When they got back to the hotel it was decided that, to save Diana's petrol, they should go on to Caldicott Manor in Harry's car, and that he should bring her back to the hotel in the late afternoon.

He drove in leisurely fashion through the winding Kent lanes which threaded over the wooded hillsides and down into the spacious valleys. It was after three o'clock before they had settled themselves in the familiar drawing room, where the afternoon sun was streaming in through a smaller window beside the fireplace.

Diana sat by the open French window and looked across the smooth lawns to the orchards beyond. A solitary blackbird perched on the low wall that enclosed the little courtyard and gazed at her curiously.

"I asked you to come down here, Diana – by the way, is it okay to call you Diana?"

"Of course. What were you saying?"

"I was going to say that I wanted to see you because I've been thinking pretty hard about what you said about your brother –"

"And about Carl Kranston?"

"That's right. Especially Carl Kranston. I feel that if he really is this fellow Grey Moose who's behind all these big robberies, then you ought to tell Sir Richard McKendrick all about it."

"He'd never believe me," she said.

"Don't be too sure about that. Sir Richard's listened to a heck of a lot of stories in his day, and he only got to his present job by being able to sort out the truth more than once in a while. He's no fool."

"But they don't even believe David was murdered," she declared impulsively. "You heard the statements at the Inquest. And when I talked to Inspector Rymer afterwards he obviously seemed to think I had a bee in my bonnet."

Harry lazily reached out for an ashtray. "Supposing," he said quietly, "that I have a certain amount of proof – enough to satisfy me, at any rate – that your brother was murdered?"

"You mean you can prove it to them?"

He hesitated. "It's a small point," he said at length. "But it seems to be pretty convincing."

"Well?"

"Why should your brother want change for a pound when he'd charged the drinks to me and had over eight shillings in loose change in his trouser pocket?"

Diana's smooth forehead furrowed in thought.

"And there's just one more point," said Harry, "that calls for a little clearing up."

"What's that?"

"Your brother was holding that gun in his left hand."

"That's true," she agreed, looking puzzled. "But David was left-handed."

"Of course he was."

"I don't see what you're getting at."

"I'm trying to tell you, Diana – your brother was murdered by someone with a little too much imagination and not quite enough intelligence. You didn't identify the body, but I can tell you that your brother never inflicted that wound on himself. It was physically impossible."

She rose to her feet in some agitation. "Why are you telling me this, Harry? If my brother was murdered why do the police think it was suicide?"

"Hold your horses, honey!" said Harry quietly. "Maybe the police ain't so sure about that suicide after all."

"But it's been in all the newspapers, and even at the Inquest they never even asked for an adjournment."

"All the same, I've got a hunch they aren't satisfied."

"Then why don't they *do* something?"

Harry shrugged. "I guess they've got their own ways of working," he hazarded. "Maybe they're not the F.B.I.'s ways, but you've got some mighty peculiar laws in this country that are liable to trip up anybody, including the police, if they don't keep to strict procedure. I dare say they've a pretty good reason for holding off a murder charge just yet awhile – there's a chance they may be waiting to get two birds with one stone. It doesn't always pay to call the bluff too soon when you're dealing with some of these crooked characters. They're liable to hop a plane and vanish."

"Yes," she mused quietly, almost to herself. "Carl Kranston has done that before now."

The door opened to admit Miles carrying a heavily loaded tea tray. They noticed that it was after five o'clock.

"On the table by the window," said Harry.

The butler set down the tray and quietly withdrew.

Harry eyed the tea tray somewhat quizzically and said to his visitor, "I can't get used to this afternoon tea set-up. Maybe you wouldn't mind …"

"Of course," smiled Diana, taking up the milk jug, and pulling the cups and saucers towards her. "How do you like it?"

"I guess it's all much the same to me. Pretty strong and fairly sweet. I tried suggesting to Miles that he should give me coffee, but I thought he'd pass through the floor!"

Diana laughed and dropped two lumps of sugar into his cup. "You'll get used to our quaint old English customs in time," she assured him.

Harry sipped his tea and pulled a face. "By the way, did you notice that quaint old customer at the Inquest?" he asked.

"You mean the little old man who was staying at the Kingfisher – what was his name?"

"Benjamin Dancey. He's a sort of antiquarian, specialising in old inns, but dabbling in anything ancient that he happens to come across. Quite a character."

"You don't think he had any connection …" She hesitated.

"He could have, I suppose. He was the only other person in the place except Bates and his wife, so far as we know."

"I've a feeling we don't know everything by a long way," she said grimly.

He passed her a plate of home-made scones, then said quietly, "I noticed something about the Kingfisher that rang a bell somewhere. In fact, it was old Dancey who indirectly drew my attention to it. Try another of those scones …" He passed the jam, helped himself to another scone, then went on thoughtfully, "If you read the reports of the robberies at Preston and Gloucester that gelignite gang pulled off, there was a man killed each time. And before they died each man whispered the words 'Grey Moose'. Your brother had been telling me about it that night he came to see me …"

"Yes, I know about Grey Moose," interposed the girl. "David said he was quite sure Carl Kranston was using that name over here. He's taken to using names like that recently – in Canada he was known as The Spider; in Brazil they called him Black Visor. David always used to say he liked those

74

fancy names because he was very vain and it made him sound daredevil and romantic. It also helped him to command a certain amount of respect among his supporters. Some of them never knew his real name, so they couldn't give him away if the police questioned them."

"The more I hear of that customer," mused Harry, "the less I like him."

"He's a danger to any civilised community," said the girl, and the note of bitterness in her voice was more pronounced than it had been. Then she suddenly became conscious of her duties and asked if he would like some more tea.

"No, sir!" he exclaimed piously, reaching for a cigarette, then replacing it in the box when he noticed that his guest had not finished. "About this Grey Moose …" he went on. "Over at the Kingfisher they hold a weekly meeting of the Antediluvian Order of Bison in a special club room."

"There's nothing very unusual about that," commented Diana. "Most of these pubs are headquarters for Buffs or Foresters or some queer society."

"Hold your horses, honey," begged Harry. "The point about this set-up is that it's called the Grey Moose Lodge. Now, does that strike a chord?"

"Grey Moose Lodge …" she repeated, her eyes widening the merest fraction. "You think they might be meeting under the cloak of these Bison or whatever they call themselves?"

"Stranger things have happened," said Harry. "Looks to me as if it would be a pretty good cover."

"Couldn't Scotland Yard keep the inn under observation?"

"Surely. The place is swarming with plain-clothes men. Inspector Bowen's hovering around too – Rymer has handed over to him."

"Inspector Bowen? Oh, yes, he was working on the case with David. Is he a friend of yours?"

"Not so's you'd notice it," grinned Harry. "We've had one or two friendly arguments in the past. Still, I got a soft spot for Michael Horatio Bowen! He's unorthodox – we've got that in common. Maybe if he hadn't been quite so rude to his superiors he'd have been a really big shot!"

"Did you go inside this club room?" she inquired, a note of eagerness in her tone.

"Oh, yes, I made George Bates unlock it. He didn't seem very pleased. But we didn't find anything in there, except the coat of arms, or whatever they call it, and some chairs and a table. And a lot of robes and chains and things in a large cupboard. It didn't get us very far, but I still have a hunch that ..."

Harry broke off as the telephone rang in the hall, and excusing himself he went out to answer it. When he returned there was a fresh glint in his eyes.

"I'll be coming back to Town with you," he announced. "That was the Assistant Commissioner. He says he particularly wants to see me."

She replaced her cup and saucer on the tray and said with some deliberation, "Harry, does this mean you're really going to work with the police?"

He shrugged. "Maybe – maybe not. I guess we'll both be pulling in the same direction. Whether we use the same tactics is anybody's guess."

"Was that the Assistant Commissioner himself on the phone?"

"It was."

"He must have been very persuasive."

"Not particularly. He just gave me a bit of news." He paused for a moment, then added in a casual tone, "There's been a big robbery at Brighton, and it seems they've left another card around with my name on it."

"Another robbery?" she exclaimed anxiously. "Harry, what does this mean?"

"It means," replied Harry Denver emphatically, "that this affair is getting beyond a joke!"

CHAPTER EIGHT

Those pioneers who exploited the health-giving effects of sea bathing on Brighton's placid beaches would, no doubt, have been slightly startled to see the fungus urban growth which resulted, and the endless surge of traffic that snaked its way towards the town every Saturday afternoon.

Brighton's early-closing habits are somewhat erratic. A section of the shops close on Wednesdays for their weekly half-holiday, others on Thursdays, and some on Saturdays. Dollands was a large Jewish family business which had always closed on Saturdays, and Grey Moose had selected it partly for this reason. It was also in a suitable position for his purpose, for it stood in the lower half of West Street below the ornate clock tower and about half-way down a fairly steep incline.

Leaving herself plenty of time to spare, Sally Harrison insinuated the long bonnet of her sports Harman-Grade into the stream of Brighton bound traffic just beyond Purley, and swept along the trunk road at a steady forty miles an hour.

As she was well ahead of time she turned off the main road just outside the town and was presently meandering through the well kept Regency squares in Hove. But she paid little attention to that dignified architecture; her brain was busy with the details of the adventure ahead. It seemed foolproof whichever way she looked at it. Every item had been checked and double-checked; everybody concerned knew exactly what he had to do.

They had all gone to Brighton by different routes at various times, so there could be very little risk of their being seen together. Moreover, the odds were that the local police would be scattered and very busily occupied with the traffic on a Saturday afternoon.

Sally steered the car on to the smooth tarmac of the promenade and sniffed the tang of the salt air appreciatively. She was feeling beautifully keyed-up now, ready for any emergency. The six cylinders of the sports car purred with a suggestion of the eighty miles an hour they could produce in a matter of seconds …

Presently she turned left into the town, and the clock at the crossroads pointed to exactly twenty-five minutes to three as she slid to the side of the rose-tinted pavement just round the corner of North Street and throttled down the powerful engine until it was barely audible. This done, she sat back and took a cigarette from her small handbag. There was not the slightest trace of emotion in her smooth, immobile features. Even when the bulky form of a policeman stopped beside the car she showed no sign of alarm.

The Constable cleared his throat and said, a little gruffly, "Sorry, Miss, you can't park here."

Sally switched on her most seductive smile. He was a very young policeman. "It's all right, officer, I'm only waiting for a friend inside the shop," she pleaded, indicating a men's outfitting establishment.

But PC Talbot was not shaken off as easily as that; he had strict instructions about parking cars in the main streets. Some of these weekend trippers thought nothing of drawing into the kerb for half an hour while the family went off for a bathe. Of course, this exquisite young blonde was obviously no weekend tripper but the Sergeant invariably saw these things in rather a different light. "There's a parking place just across the square, Miss," he said persuasively.

"But my friend promised he wouldn't be more than two minutes, and if I go off to a car park he won't have the least idea where I am." Her eyes seemed large and luminous and eloquent in their appeal.

PC Talbot hesitated. "It won't have to be for more than a couple of minutes, then, Miss," he stipulated. "You wouldn't believe the trouble we have with this lot on a Saturday." With an expressive nod he indicated the crowds of holiday-makers surging down towards the Parade.

"I'm sure I don't know how you manage to cope with them," said Sally admiringly in her most melting tones. "I was only telling my friend this morning that the police of this country are dreadfully underpaid for the work they do and all the risks they have to take."

She smiled at him a trifle wistfully, and PC Talbot felt for a moment that a policeman's lot was not entirely an unhappy one. "Oh, it's not as bad as all that, Miss," he said with a deprecating grin. "Mind you, I'm not saying we couldn't do with another pound or two ..."

He broke off suddenly and straightened himself as there were unmistakable sounds of confusion coming from the upper part of West Street. In the distance, and growing rapidly louder, was the strident blast of a motor horn. People were scattering in all directions to the safety of doorways and shop entries. A young woman pushing a pram screamed and rushed off down North Street with a scurry of flying heels.

The Constable moved towards the crossroads, but before he had gone many yards the lorry came into sight, swaying drunkenly, far above the regulation speed. It was an old-fashioned five-tonner, which still had some traces of green paint on its body. To a casual observer it seemed obvious that the brakes had failed and the vehicle was completely out of the driver's control.

Talbot caught his breath as the lorry seemed almost certain to rush full tilt into the clock tower. But the driver somehow contrived to send it skidding past, and with yet another violent lurch it came jolting over the incline into the lower part of the street which was fairly free from traffic, though a small stream of cars had just that moment turned in from the promenade.

It seemed that the sight of these oncoming cars urged the lorry driver to a sudden decision, and he turned his front wheels into the kerb as if to check the vehicle. But the wheels mounted the pavement and with a deafening clatter the bonnet crashed straight through the plate glass window of the gown shop next door to Dollands the jewellers. The driver was seen to shield his face with his elbow as splinters of wood and glass flew in all directions. Torn dresses and dainty lingerie were draped grotesquely over the bonnet of the lorry, and two particularly elegantly dressed models were tilted tipsily against the driver's cabin.

An elderly lady, who looked like the proprietress, and an assistant cowered helplessly behind the partition which divided the shop from a small office. They clung to each other, speechless from shock.

Now the pedestrians began running from the openings and shop entrances where they had taken cover – luckily there had been no one near the dress shop – and they surged round the scene of the accident, ignoring PC Talbot's well-meaning attempt to clear the pavement. Someone rushed off to telephone for an ambulance, and above the din of the motor horn another man was heard to shout something about the driver.

"Out of the way there! Out of my way!" called PC Talbot for the tenth time as he elbowed his way through the crowd. But most of the spectators stood their ground with the morbid expectation of some grisly spectacle which seems to grip so many onlookers.

This time, however, they were to be disappointed. Indeed, the least perturbed person present was the driver, who slowly forced open the door of his cab and clambered down quite unhurt. The Constable yelled something at him but he did not seem to hear. Standing amongst the shambles of torn dresses he reached into his cabin for a screwdriver, then with the policeman's help he managed to lift the bonnet, and after a minute or two the din from the horn abruptly ceased. It was replaced by the clang of a burglar alarm.

"It was the brakes, Constable – I only got the lorry yesterday, and they told me they were all in order – the swine!" Sam was complaining. He broke off for a second, knowing only too well what was the cause of the bell. He tried to divert the Constable's attention. "I must have bashed through the wires of the burglar alarm," he said quickly, and the officer nodded.

Talbot went over to the women in the office and called out above the din, "You all right?" The older woman nodded rather dubiously, and Talbot cupped his hands and shouted, "Can't you switch off that bell?"

The woman shook her head tearfully, disclaiming all knowledge of the source of the commotion. In another second the Constable would have realised that the noise came from the next door, but at that moment the ambulance came rushing up with yet another bell reverberating heavily, and bringing an extra fifty or sixty spectators rushing behind it. By this time the crowd had swelled into the roadway and was seriously threatening to hold up the traffic. Two more policemen arrived on the scene and began to push back the people while Talbot assured the ambulance men that their services were not required after all.

Sam Crawford leaned against the lorry, looking somewhat dazed, and Talbot started to take down some details in his notebook. Sam purposely hesitated in answering the questions, hedging now and then, and talking much more than was necessary.

By now the other two policemen had realised that it was the jewellers' alarm bell that was ringing, but they did not attach any serious importance to it. They readily accepted the theory that the terrific jolt to the adjacent premises was entirely responsible. One of them went to telephone the private house of one of the partners while the other climbed up and muffled the clapper of the bell with a large handkerchief.

The clock in the tower pointed to three-forty-five as Joe Wilcox emerged from a side alley in North Street and handed Sally a cheap brown attaché case.

"Everything okay?" she asked.

"It was a hell of a crash," he whispered, looking round furtively. "I hope Sam was all right."

"Don't worry about that," she advised, stowing the case under the front seat. "You get off back there as quickly as you can."

He nodded and slammed the car door. There was hardly anyone in sight as Sally slammed the gears and the car reared off.

Joe watched the car until it disappeared from sight, then turned and made for the crowd which was still surging round the dress shop.

He displayed such enthusiasm for his new role of curious onlooker that PC Talbot singled him out almost at once and thrust a restraining elbow across his chest. "Here you, take it easy! It's folk like you who make all the trouble!" the Constable declared with unconscious irony.

CHAPTER NINE

The fact that they each possessed a car was introducing a chain of complications into the lives of Diana Stone and Harry Denver in that they desired nothing so much as to travel in the same car together.

On the evening of the Brighton robbery they were anxious to return to London in such intimate fashion, but it was only after a considerable amount of discussion that they finally evolved a plan. Harry was to take them to Sevenoaks in his car, which he would park at the hotel. From there they would travel to Town in Diana's, and he would spend the night at the St. Regis, as it looked like being a late session at the Yard.

She invited him to lunch at her flat the following day, conscious that it was high time she returned some of his elaborate hospitality, and she had already telephoned her housekeeper, Mrs Bentley, to warn her that there would be company to lunch. They hadn't quite decided how Harry would get back to Sevenoaks but he assured her that there was an excellent train service, and hundreds of hire cars available in the event of an emergency.

They started almost at once, and as they slowed down to emerge from the gates of the Manor into the main road a shining Harman-Grade sports car swept past and the girl at the wheel raised an indolent hand in greeting.

"Friend of yours?" inquired Diana, hoping her voice sounded more indifferent than she felt.

"Sort of," grinned Harry. "More of a neighbour really. She's the niece of the doctor who lives along the way at a house called White Towers. I fish in their pond once in a while."

"She's a very attractive girl," persisted Diana.

"I guess so," replied Harry without enthusiasm.

"Don't you agree?"

"I operated too long in night-club circles maybe …
Anyhow, I seem to be kind of allergic to blondes nowadays.
They don't remind me of zephyrs in the cornfield any more."

She laughed, then looked thoughtful. "I'm sure I've seen
that girl before somewhere," she murmured as they came into
the outskirts of Sevenoaks. "I wish I could think where."

"Probably at some dress show, or maybe a party," he
suggested. "I dare say you get around quite a bit in that job of
yours. You must tell me more about it some time. I'm such a
lazy so-and-so I enjoy hearing how people work for a living."

She looked at him for a moment, then said with a slow
smile, "You don't fool me, Mr Denver."

"Honey, I'd be scared even to try," he solemnly assured
her as he manoeuvred the car towards the hotel garage.

With Diana driving her own car they were heading for
London five minutes later, and as there was comparatively
little traffic until they approached the more thickly populated
South London area they did the journey in remarkably good
time.

"Where would you like me to drop you?" she asked as
they crossed Lambeth Bridge.

"But you're not shaking me off just like that," he
protested. "I guess I'll be needing you as an alibi. You're
about the only person who can testify that I haven't been into
any mischief all afternoon."

She hesitated a moment, then said, "Oh very well, if you
really think it's as serious as all that."

"But it is," he insisted. "Didn't I tell you they'd found
another of those cards with my name on it?"

"You didn't tell me very much else about this Brighton
affair," she reminded him.

"Because the Yard weren't doing much talking over the
phone. You know as much as I do about it." He paused for a
moment, then said hesitantly, "Of course, if you had a date for

85

this evening … well, I guess they won't gaol me for a day or two."

Diana smiled. "I'd hate to see anything like that happen to you," she said. "Are you going straight to the Yard?"

He nodded, and she swung the car in an easterly direction along the Westminster Embankment.

"Grey Moose seems to be quite determined to blow my small reputation to shreds," ruminated Harry as he watched her steer her way deftly between two buses.

"Have you upset him in any way in the past, do you think?"

"I don't even know the guy! But there's always a chance I might have pulled a fast one across one of his buddies. That's the worst of keeping bad company, it's liable to catch up on you when you least expect it," he told her seriously. "You might care to remember that and put it in your column some time when you're writing a piece about juvenile delinquents."

"I'll keep that in mind," she promised as she steered into position in a line of cars parked in a side road near the Yard.

Harry was laboriously extricating his large feet when he noticed a familiar figure emerging from the next car but one ahead. "Hi there, Bowen!" he called.

The sturdy young man in his middle thirties turned and recognised Harry at once.

Inspector Michael Horatio Bowen would not have been readily recognised as a plain-clothes detective, a factor which had proved a considerable assistance to him in his career. He was well dressed in a dark suit which set off his trim masculine figure to its best advantage.

Harry introduced him to Diana and at once Bowen was on the alert.

"You're the woman who writes for the *Daily Messenger*?" he queried, for Bowen always believed in keeping in with the Press, holding the theory that carefully controlled publicity could go a long way to smashing any crime racket. He was even ready to make friends with the editor of a boys' comic paper just in case he might come in useful one day.

Diana acknowledged her Fleet Street connections and Bowen immediately suggested that they should adjourn to the tavern nearby for a drink.

"They're expecting me at the Yard," Harry told him.

"You mean about the Brighton job?" said Bowen. "Yes, I'm due for that little pow-wow as well. They can do without us for ten minutes while we give each other the low-down."

"Have you come from Brighton then?" asked Harry as the Inspector led them to the pub in question.

"No, I've come from near your place at Sevenoaks. I've been keeping a pretty close watch on the Kingfisher. So close, in fact, that I haven't had a chance to call in on you."

They found a fairly remote table in a corner of the lounge and a barman came and took their order for drinks.

"I've telephoned you twice, Harry, to find out just how far you were involved in this business," said Bowen, having made sure they could not be overheard.

"Looks to me like I'm in it just up to the ears," said Harry. "So is Miss Stone here." He went on to give the Inspector a brief outline of everything that concerned them, and Bowen eyed Diana with new respect.

"So you're Falconer's sister, eh? Your brother was a great scout, Miss Stone! He did me a couple of good turns in my early days, and I haven't forgotten. I'd hoped to pay him back some time; now it seems the only thing I can do is to get the swine who shot him."

"Then you think it was murder?" she queried eagerly.

"It was murder all right!" declared Bowen confidently. "We're pretty sure of that over at the Yard, though we can't prove anything – yet. But I don't like the look of that

Kingfisher place. I don't like the landlord, nor some of the characters I've seen hanging around there."

"Such as?" put in Harry casually.

"Well, one of my men bumped into a cove named Sam Crawford there yesterday. Just caught a glimpse of him going out of the back door, then he seems to have vanished."

"Sam Crawford?" repeated Harry. "I remember him – he used to be a film stunt man – then something to do with a travelling fair – and since then he's been mixed up with one or two smash-and-grab set-ups. Used to have the nerve of the devil himself!"

"You've got a pretty good memory, Harry," said Bowen, eyeing him shrewdly.

"Absolutely card index!" Harry assured him cheerfully. "It's the best thing a feller can have when he's in my racket."

"And what's your racket now?"

"I'm not operating at the moment," grinned Harry, refusing to be drawn. "But it looks as if I'll soon be pulled into something pretty big, and on the side of law and order for once in a way." He lifted his glass. "Well, here's to the spice of life!"

"What would Sam Crawford be doing in the heart of Kent?" he went on presently. "I guess that's a pretty serious question you should ask yourself, Inspector – and here's hoping you get the right answer. Your man should have tailed him."

"He didn't get a chance," said the Inspector. "There wasn't a sign of him after he went out of the back door. And, of course, the landlord had never heard of him."

"I don't trust that landlord," said Harry, and went on to relate the incident concerning the changing of Falconer's pound note.

Bowen frowned thoughtfully when he had finished, then said, "It's beginning to dawn on me why they've picked on you for a sort of scapegoat, old man."

"You mean this gang are probably using the Kingfisher as headquarters," put in Diana, "and they think that if it should be traced, then the fact that Harry lives nearby will –"

"Will immediately arouse the suspicions of the police," Bowen finished for her. "You're pretty smart, Miss Stone. That's exactly what I was thinking. Nobody could be blamed for putting such an obvious two and two together."

Harry broke open a packet of Chesterfields and passed them round. "It certainly looks like I've got to play in with you boys for once in a while," he said presently. "I've been trying hard this last week to think of some other way, but this Grey Moose seems to have 'em all nicely sealed off."

Bowen thumped his fist on the table. "Certainly you've got to help us, Harry. And there's Miss Stone here; we've got to keep an eye on her. If Grey Moose finds out about her …"

"Did you check on that little guy named Dancey?" put in Harry hastily, anxious that Diana should not be in any way alarmed.

"Oh yes," replied Bowen. "He seems all above board as far as I can make out. He's a retired prep school master – lives alone in a Bayswater flatlet. Spends a lot of time at the British Museum, so he told me. Calls himself an antiquarian."

"That might cover a multitude of sins," murmured Harry. "For instance, he might be mugging up ancient Egyptian poisons that could come in handy, or –"

"He said he was mainly interested in English inns, though he's lately been dabbling in Roman villas," grinned the Inspector. "I think he's a pretty harmless old bird myself."

"You wouldn't have been reading *Goodbye Mr Chips* just lately?" queried Harry, with the merest twitch of his expressive mouth, and Diana caught his eye and smiled.

"You've got to admit," he continued, "that it's queer the old boy should be on the spot the night of that murder. They don't get a guest at the Kingfisher once in three months, except right in the middle of the summer, so the locals tell me." He signalled the barman to bring another round of drinks. "I guess we've got to think twice before we write off the old boy as harmless."

Bowen stubbed out his cigarette. "Have it your own way, Harry," he grunted. "I'll have the boys keep an eye on him. We can't afford to leave anything to chance. All the same, if that old bird's a master criminal I'll pack up and go and lecture at Hendon!"

Harry laughed. "I don't reckon things are quite as bad as that, Inspector. But I'd like to know what's been going on at Brighton this afternoon. Sir Richard wouldn't say much on the phone."

"It's in the stop press of most of the evening papers," said Bowen. "Though they haven't got the full story by any means. It seems the gang decided to try their hand at a daylight job for a change, and they got away with it very nicely. It must have been pretty thoroughly planned, right down to the last detail."

"Any idea how much stuff was there?"

Bowen looked round cautiously, then dropped his voice. "Getting on for eighty thousand pounds, Sir Richard said when he phoned me. It was Dollands, the jewellers, and they were carrying a much bigger stock than usual. They've had several apparently genuine inquiries during the past week for expensive rings and necklaces, so naturally they got the stuff from Town for approval. It was all worked out very neatly, including a lorry crashing into the shop next door to cover the noise when they blew the safe."

"Pretty smart," commented Harry, taking a gulp of his whisky.

"And it seems they even had time to plant one of your cards before they made a getaway."

"Not one of my cards," Harry corrected him. "A card with my name on it that I didn't pay for. And you needn't give me that funny look, Inspector, because I can quite easily prove that I was at home all afternoon."

"Glad to hear it, old man," said Bowen, though there was a trace of false heartiness in his voice.

"I'm getting a little tired," went on Harry, "of having to establish alibis like that. Maybe there'll come a time when they'll pull one of these jobs on a day when I spent the whole time by myself fishing. Then I'll be in a spot! This business is getting on my nerves, and I object to anything that gets on my nerves. I'm kinda touchy about little things like that." He lit a cigarette and thoughtfully watched a cloud of tobacco smoke rise towards the ceiling.

"Inspector," Diana said suddenly, "What's happened to the driver of that lorry that smashed into the shop?"

Harry came abruptly back to earth. "Yes, Inspector, what's happened to that driver?"

"Sir Richard said he got away when the police were coping with the crowd. They took his name and address –"

"That'll be phoney," said Harry quickly. "Come on, Inspector, we'd better get round to the Yard. There's no time to be lost!"

"What are you up to, Harry?" Bowen looked puzzled.

"It stands out like Cleopatra's Needle!" said Harry Denver. "Hurry up, Inspector – I think a special 'all stations' call seems to be indicated."

"An 'all stations' call?" repeated Bowen obviously bewildered.

"Sure, Inspector – for a stunt man named Sam Crawford!"

CHAPTER TEN

Without any further delay Bowen led his visitors through the front hall of New Scotland Yard and along various corridors past the famous Information Room, with its three brilliantly lighted sections, to a room where a battery of teleprinters was busy clicking.

Bowen phoned Brighton to check Sam Crawford's description and a few minutes later they were sending it over to a hundred principal stations.

"That's that!" declared Bowen with a sigh of relief. "Now we'll go upstairs and see Sir Richard."

The Assistant Commissioner was alone in his office, engaged on what appeared to be an important telephone conversation, and he motioned to them to be seated. When he eventually replaced the receiver Bowen introduced him to Diana and gave him a brief account of her connection to the case. As soon as he heard that she was Falconer's sister Sir Richard leaned forward in his chair and listened with keen interest. Presently he opened a drawer and produced a silver cigarette box which he handed round, and two minutes later Diana told her story for the third time.

Sir Richard made a note or two and asked her an occasional question. Once or twice he prompted her on minor matters, but for the main part she spoke without interruption. Towards the end of her story the Assistant Commissioner opened a file and cross-checked several facts that she had mentioned, nodding quietly as he did so.

"That's very interesting, Miss Stone … very interesting," he murmured as she finished her story and stubbed out her cigarette with a hand that was shaking slightly. There had been traces of emotion in her voice when she spoke of her brother and it was obvious to McKendrick that she was completely sincere.

He looked at her shrewdly for a few seconds, then said, "You seem quite certain that from the very beginning your brother was under the impression that the brains behind these robberies was Carl Kranston."

"Quite sure, Sir Richard," she replied with quiet emphasis.

He stroked his chin thoughtfully. "I admit that Falconer seemed very positive about this being an elaborate criminal organisation, but he never said anything about Carl Kranston."

"He wanted to be quite certain first," she answered. "You see, he had no evidence against Kranston … not even a photograph. He knew what a devil the man is, and he had to go very carefully."

There was silence for a moment, then the Assistant Commissioner swung round in his seat. "What do you make of all this, Mr Denver? Have you ever come across Carl Kranston in your wide and varied experience?"

Harry grinned and shook his head. "No, sir, but I heard quite a bit about him in the States. I guess he gave the F.B.I. boys a few headaches before he cleaned up fifty thousand dollars in some big Wall Street affair and vanished the next day. Yes, this Carl is quite a character!"

"That doesn't necessarily mean that he's running this organisation."

"That's quite true," said Harry. "But it looks mighty like it to me. Falconer was convinced about it in his own mind, and Falconer was murdered all right."

Sir Richard looked up sharply. "What makes you so certain about that?"

"Falconer was holding the revolver in his left hand," Harry said, "but he'd been shot through the opposite side of his head. Falconer was left-handed all right, but I wouldn't say he was a contortionist into the bargain."

"True enough," agreed the Assistant Commissioner at once. "I've been meaning to ask you about that doctor fellow who gave evidence, Denver. Is he a neighbour of yours?"

"Oh, yes," replied Harry. "He was dining with me that evening."

"You know him well?"

"I wouldn't say that."

"H'm … well, I've looked into the *Medical Directory*, and there doesn't seem to be any trace of him there."

"I believe he took his degrees somewhere abroad," said Harry. "He tells me he spent a lot of time on the Gold Coast."

"H'm! Well, he certainly seems to have made a mess of this job. Any damned fool could see with half an eye that it wasn't suicide! There wasn't even a trace of a burn near the wound."

"Perhaps I shouldn't say this," began Harry, "but the doc had been drinking pretty heavily that night – and he had one or two more at the Kingfisher. He was certainly mellow."

"Oh, well, perhaps that explains it." Sir Richard shrugged. "All the same, it was most unfortunate."

Harry smiled lazily. "Maybe it'll work out better than he thought."

"Meaning what, exactly?"

"Well, if the gang take it for granted that the police have accepted the suicide verdict they're liable to relax their defences … and nobody in their position can afford to relax."

The Assistant Commissioner nodded approvingly. "Yes, you're right there, Denver. I don't propose to reopen the case of Falconer's death until we've got the man who killed him. You agree with that, Miss Stone?"

"Oh, yes, Sir Richard."

"When did you last see your brother?"

"Shortly before he visited Mr Denver."

"Did he seem cheerful and in normal health?"

"Much the same as usual. He was worried about this case, of course, but he didn't seem depressed at all. We never saw very much of each other, Sir Richard. My work kept me very busy, and he was often in and out of Town."

"Yes, of course."

McKendrick made several more notes, then, as he seemed to have completed his questioning, Bowen quietly intervened and told him about the all-stations call for Sam Crawford. Sir Richard nodded his approval and began sorting through the contents of his grey folder.

Harry looked across at Diana, gave an uneasy smile, and shuffled his feet. "Sir Richard," he said at last, "why did you ask me to come here tonight?"

The Assistant Commissioner deliberately closed his folder and placed it on one side. "I've been waiting for you to ask me that, Mr Denver," he replied in a pleasant tone. "Why do you think I invited you?"

"In the first place," Harry hazarded, "I'd say you wanted to make sure I had a good alibi for this afternoon. Well, there she is." He nodded across at Diana. "We've spent the entire afternoon together since one-thirty."

"Is that correct, Miss Stone?"

"Quite correct, Sir Richard. And if you want another witness there's Mr Denver's butler."

A vestige of a smile flickered across McKendrick's deeply-lined features. "So you run to a butler nowadays, Denver?"

"A very respectable butler, Sir Richard," replied Harry imperturbably. "He'd be quite horrified if he knew where I was at this minute."

Sir Richard permitted himself a grim chuckle. "All right, Denver. I always suspected those cards were deliberately planted. Now, I want to talk to you two in complete confidence. Can you forget about that newspaper of yours for ten minutes, Miss Stone?"

"I'm only interested in seeing my brother's murderer punished, Sir Richard," she solemnly assured him.

"And I'm gunning for the guy who's trying to roll my name in the mud," put in Harry. "'He who steals my purse steals trash, but he that filches from me my good name …'"

"All right," interrupted McKendrick hastily. "Well, I don't mind admitting to you that this case is getting us pretty badly rattled. We never know quite where this gang will break out next and what method they'll use. The man – or woman – at the head seems to be able to put his finger on all the weak spots in the police organisation. In fact, they're apparently a couple of moves ahead of us the whole time." He picked up a briar pipe from his inkstand and began to fill it slowly from a tin which stood on his desk. "… This is only a vague sort of idea of mine, Denver," he went on with some hesitation. "But I know you're a pretty unorthodox type, and you've a fairly wide knowledge of what the Sunday papers call the underworld. Now, I gather you're quite keen to help us on this case, and I thought if we gave you a free hand …" He placed the lid on the tin very carefully. "How does that strike you?"

"Are you suggesting I should turn into a glorified – er – copper's nark, I think you call it over here?" queried Harry.

"I'm prepared to leave the plan of campaign to you. We'll either work with you or quite independently, whichever suits you better."

"You embarrass me, Sir Richard," said Harry. "I'd sure like to help, but I haven't any plan of campaign right now, except to keep a close watch on the Kingfisher and ask a guy named Sam Crawford a few awkward questions as soon as I can lay hands on him."

"Later, perhaps," nodded the Assistant Commissioner. "At the moment, I'm particularly anxious to discover how the gang gets the stuff out of the country – as they must be doing, because if it were still here we'd have it tracked down within a couple of days. Isn't that so, Bowen?"

"That's so, sir," the Inspector agreed.

"Now, that's one direction where you might come in useful, Denver," continued the Assistant Commissioner. "You're pretty used to picking up information about the valuable piece of jewellery floating around the world. There was that affair of the Berkeley rubies, for instance; that very nearly landed you into a pretty mess!"

"It landed the man who stole them into a prettier one," Harry reminded him. "I'm sorry, sir," he went on, "but I'm a bit out of touch with such goings-on these days. But maybe I'll take a look around one of these fine evenings and see what I can pick up."

There was a soft buzz and Sir Richard lifted one of the telephone receivers on his desk. He listened for a moment, then gave a couple of brisk orders and replaced the instrument.

He turned to Harry and said, "You wanted a few words with Sam Crawford?"

"I'll say I do!"

"All right, then, be here at ten sharp in the morning. They've just picked him up near Purley."

***

With the rest of the evening to themselves Harry and Diana summoned a taxi in the Charing Cross Road, having decided it was rather too late to go to the theatre. Harry persuaded her to accompany him to a small club near the Marble Arch which he knew well enough to secure admission without any difficulty.

"You may see one or two characters there you could put in your column. I guess they'd be tickled to death!" he grinned, adding that there was no necessity for either of them to dress for the occasion. "They've got a chef there who really knows his way around," he concluded as a final recommendation.

As its name implied, The Bouquets Club had a late-Victorian atmosphere, with gilt and cupids very much in evidence.

In a far corner, surrounded by several palms, a trio of demurely dressed young ladies dispensed Victorian melodies on piano, violin, and cello.

"There's something kinda restful about this place," murmured Harry as he passed the menu over to Diana. "Other folks must find it so as well, because some of the biggest crooked deals of all time have been cooked up here. Mind you, the place is strictly above-board; never been raided once, or I wouldn't have brought you."

"I appreciate your thoughtfulness, Mr Denver," replied Diana in a serious tone, though there was a suspicion of a twinkle in the grey eyes.

A waiter came and took their order and Diana nodded to a couple of people he knew. He began to describe some of the diners to her.

"The blonde dripping with ice over by the door," – he indicated a glittering fair-haired woman laden with jewels on every visible extremity – "she's tied up with a nice little racket in luxury flats. Started as a typist in an estate office; in next to no time the boss had taken a fancy to her – his wife divorced him – the blonde became more expensive – he had to start racketeering to pay her bills – and now she owns the business. It just shows what a girl can do if she keeps her wits about her!"

"Oh dear," said Diana. "And I get so many letters from typists telling me the boss is in love with them. I'm beginning to wonder if I was right in advising them to look for another job."

"You bet you were right!" replied Harry emphatically, nodding in the blonde's direction. "I wouldn't have a dog of mine step into her shoes."

A stocky young man in a much too tightly fitting suit wandered over to the blonde's table and seated himself with a possessive air.

"Small-time crook," explained Harry. "There's no depths a woman of that type can't sink to. *And* he's kept her waiting at least twenty minutes."

A waited stepped on to the orchestra's rostrum and whispered something to the leader. Presently they burst into a tinkling version of a famous galop.

"That's one of Tommy Belton's favourites – he's a sucker for Offenbach," murmured Harry, turning in his chair to get a glimpse of the man in question, a well groomed elderly business man in the late fifties. Harry pointed him out to Diana as he applauded heartily at the end of the piece.

"He looks very respectable," she commented.

"He's never been found out yet," was the cryptic reply. "Tommy has a very cosy little motor showroom in Great Portland Street, but nobody's ever yet managed to discover how he keeps a luxury flat in Park Lane, a large house near Ascot, a string of racehorses, and an equally expensive string of girlfriends."

"Maybe he's discovered a new way of dodging super-tax," suggested Diana.

"Say, I hope you're not going to print any of this in your column," put in Harry hastily, with vivid recollections of the American yellow press.

"There's such a thing as a law of libel," she reminded him. "And in any case, mine is a highly respectable column."

"I guess I asked for that one," he murmured as the waiter placed the celebrated chicken *à la* king before them.

Suddenly, from behind the waiter, the figure of an energetic man in his early forties loomed up and tapped Harry on the shoulder.

"Hi, Harry! Where have you been hiding yourself lately?" demanded a cultured voice with just the barest trace of a foreign accent.

"Well, well!" exclaimed Harry, laying down his knife and fork. "If it isn't Max Hood! How's the world treating you?" He introduced Diana and invited the newcomer to join them.

But Hood shook his head. "Sorry, old man, I'm expecting a certain party on a little matter of business. May see you later."

And he went off to the table reserved for him, a trim figure in his dinner jacket and razor-creased trousers.

"Is he a great friend of yours?" inquired Diana as they continued their dinner.

"Nobody in this joint is a friend of mine, or anyone else's. They're not the sort of folk who make friends – only business acquaintances or sleeping partners," explained Harry patiently. "The only friendship they're capable of forming is with a wad of banknotes."

"How horrible!" said Diana with a little shudder.

"Oh, I guess you get used to it," said Harry philosophically. "They're quite interesting characters in their way, and folks have always had a kind of fascination for me. Take Max Hood, for instance …"

"You mean the man you just introduced to me?"

"That's right. Hood is something new in the crime racket, a really international 'fence'; with headquarters in half a dozen countries."

"You mean he's a receiver of stolen property?"

"In a very big way only. Hood never bothers with the small-time crooks. I doubt if he ever makes a deal for less than ten thousand. Strictly big-time, that's Hood."

"What nationality is he?"

"His father was a clock repairer in a back street in Rome; his mother was a Greek servant girl. Hood was a petty thief in Rome before the war, and during the war years he was right in the black market with both feet. The dollars that boy turned over must have upset the exchanges more than somewhat. Now he's operating across half the civilised globe; Hood's one of the penalties of civilisation! ... And don't let that smiling boy act fool you – Hood is ruthless with a capital R. He learnt it in the back alleys of Rome, and he'll never forget."

The trio began to saw and thump its way through a Strauss waltz with somewhat surprising dexterity. The leader, a brassy blonde with a generous figure and ready smile, was obviously a great favourite with the male members of the club.

"You certainly know some colourful types, Harry," smiled Diana as the waiter placed an enormous ice in front of her. "Tell me some more about Max Hood."

"I guess there isn't much to tell. He's the biggest receiver of stolen gems in the world – has his own staff to break 'em up – fake 'em up – repolish 'em – and never makes less than a hundred per cent profit. You see, all his set-ups are operated under cover of a legitimate business, and nobody's been able to prove that it was anything but above-board – yet."

"Shouldn't you tell all this to the police?" demanded Diana, wide-eyed.

"Maybe I should," chuckled Harry. "If it was as simple as all that. Maybe the police know in any case and wouldn't thank me for squeaking. Besides, there's no knowing when a guy like Hood won't come in useful. I always say there's no point in upsetting people unless there's money in it."

Diana laughed. "That's one way of looking at things."

The crowd in the club was getting thicker now; almost every table was occupied with the queerest assortment of humanity Diana had ever seen. There were dowager types who might have been Gaiety girls in their youth, thin middle-aged women with a nervous manner and abrupt gestures, and a sprinkling of very expensively dressed young ladies from gown shops, beauty establishments, and film studios, whose purpose was obviously solely to entertain and bring prestige to their male escorts.

It seemed to Diana that the conversation had a slightly sinister buzz, perhaps on account of its polyglot nature. Waiters quickened the pace to and from the kitchens, and the trio began an extract from Verdi that was quite beyond its powers.

A tall, attractive girl, beautifully dressed in a dark gown, stood in the doorway for a moment and caught Diana's eye. She watched her move to a table where Hood rose to welcome her.

As the girl sat down Diana pointed her out to Harry. "Where *have* I seen that girl before?" she asked with a puzzled little frown.

Harry whistled softly to himself as he saw Hood summon a waiter to order a drink for his guest. "You've seen her this evening," he told Diana in a tone that controlled any trace of surprise. "You saw her outside my place in a car … She's my neighbour – Sally Harrison."

CHAPTER ELEVEN

If Harry had been intrigued at the sight of a business meeting between Sally Harrison and Max Hood he certainly did not allow it to interfere with his sleep, and it was not until he heard a heavy knock at his door and a voice informing him that it was nine o'clock that he returned fully to consciousness and recalled that he was due at the Yard in an hour's time.

He went down into the dining room at the St Regis to be informed that breakfast was over, but as a great favour the waiter rescued a fillet of lukewarm sole and a couple of dejected pieces of toast for him. Coffee, it seemed, was right out of the question and orange juice unheard of. He asked for the Head Waiter to offer some protest at such hospitality, only to be told that gentleman never came on duty at breakfast. And the Manager of the hotel was busy in another part of the building. Harry gave it up, paid his account, and set out for New Scotland Yard.

There did not seem to be many taxis about on this fine Sunday morning, and Harry had a rooted objection to any more walking than was absolutely necessary. However, he eventually found one in Piccadilly and was outside the main entrance to the Yard just before ten.

He was ushered into the Assistant Commissioner's office without any delay, and discovered Sir Richard already there chatting to Bowen and Rymer. A report from the Brighton police of the previous day's affair was on McKendrick's desk and made none too pleasant reading.

"Well, what do we know about Sam Crawford?" asked Harry as soon as they had exchanged greetings.

"We're holding him on a charge of being implicated with the Brighton robbery," replied Sir Richard, "but I'm afraid it isn't going to be easy to make him talk – and if he did I'm not sure that he knows very much."

"No harm in trying," said Harry. "I see from this morning's papers that the robbery wasn't discovered until some time after the truck bashed into the shop."

"That's so," said Bowen. "Actually, whoever did the job set off the burglar alarm, but the damn fools thought it was the lorry that had jolted it. They didn't find out any different till one of the partners came along with the keys."

"I see. Has anybody tried to make him talk?"

"Yes, Bowen and Rymer have both had a go at him without very much satisfaction."

"We found the nameplate on the lorry was a fake," said Bowen, "and he won't say if he was driving it for anybody. His story is that he bought the lorry to go into business himself and the brakes were faulty. But we've had the brakes tested and they're quite okay, so it was obviously a put-up job."

"What's he say to all that?"

"He simply insists he's sticking to his statement."

Harry leaned against the window-ledge and thoughtfully watched the traffic crossing Lambeth Bridge. "There must be some way of making him talk," he reflected, almost to himself.

"We'll see," said the Assistant Commissioner. "You'd better bring him in, Rymer."

Bowen and Rymer went out, and Sir Richard turned to Harry. "How much do you think he knows?" he asked.

"Enough to break up that outfit if we can get the truth out of him," replied Harry. "Do you mind if I talk to him, Chief?"

Sir Richard hesitated. "Well, it isn't usual, but it seems we've got to use unorthodox methods on this job. We don't want any third degree stuff, mind."

"Leave it to me, sir," smiled Harry. "I'll handle him with kid gloves."

Presently the door opened and the two Inspectors reappeared with a very sullen prisoner between them. Sam looked as though he had not slept well; his hair was dishevelled, his face badly shaved, and his necktie carelessly knotted.

Rymer set down a letter-tray containing an assortment of small articles on the Assistant Commissioner's desk. "These were found in his pockets, sir," he said quietly, and Harry moved across to take a look at them while Sir Richard seated the prisoner in a chair facing the strong light from the tall window.

In the tray were a new gold cigarette case, a wallet containing a driving licence and twenty-four pound notes, as well as several faded newspaper cuttings concerning the owner's speedway exploits, a cheap postcard photograph of a girl, a dirty handkerchief, a small battered silver flask containing some sort of liquor, a large penknife, a ballpoint pen with a patent gadget for checking sparking-plugs, and a few shillings' worth of loose change.

"What the 'ell's the big idea of all this?" rasped Sam Crawford's unpleasant voice as he looked round the room with a furtive air. "I ain't a blasted criminal – I got my rights!"

Harry Denver perched on the edge of the desk. He fixed Sam with an intense stare, then smiled lazily. "Of course you've got your rights, Sam," he said softly. "There's nothing to worry about – you and I are just going to have a little talk."

Sam Crawford licked his lips nervously and again looked round the little group of immobile faces. "I got nothing to say," he stammered. "I want a solicitor here if you're askin' me questions ..."

"I tell you it's all right, Sam," Harry interposed once more. "This is just a little talk off the record. We know a bit more about this Brighton set-up than you think. It's for your own good that we're giving you this chance to tell us what you know. You're mixing with a pretty tough crowd; they've already wiped out a couple of inside men who let them down. They've no time for failures, and it looks as if you're going to need protection."

"I can look after myself," said Sam sullenly.

"I dare say the other two had the same ideas about that." There was a quiet intensity about Harry's voice that compelled attention.

Sam became more and more ill at ease; from time to time he shifted awkwardly in his chair.

"We know you're connected with the Grey Moose gang because we've seen you at the Kingfisher," Harry went on, quite unperturbed. "Was that where you planned this little coup?"

"I don't know what you're talking about."

"Oh, yes you do, Sam. Just as well as you know those pounds in your wallet are part of the proceeds from the Gloucester job. We're catching up with the Grey Moose crowd pretty fast, Sam."

"I got nothing to do with any gang!"

"Then all I can say is, I hope for your sake you're pretty fond of children."

"What the 'ell has kids got to go with this? I didn't hurt no kids!"

"I'm trying to tell you how, Sam. I said I hoped you were mighty fond of children, because this time you're the sucker who's holding the baby. And, oh boy, what a bouncing baby it is! I shouldn't wonder if your share of the rake-off came to a couple of thousand, Sam. I told you that crowd has no time for failures – all you'll get will be a bullet in the guts, the same as the lorry driver at Preston and the night watchman at Gloucester. Of course, that's assuming you manage to wriggle out of taking the rap for this job – and that isn't going to be easy. They're piling up quite a bit of evidence against you, and you've got a record that's none too healthy. I don't suppose the Judge'll feel any too brotherly towards you."

Harry paused for a moment to let Sam assimilate all the implications to the full, and he certainly seemed to find them far from comforting. He licked his lips nervously once more and ran a finger uneasily around the neck of his collar. He lowered his eyes and refused to meet Harry's unwavering gaze.

"If you know what's good for you, Sam," continued the soft, remorseless voice, "you'll start talking right now. You've nothing to lose except your cut on that job and you'll never get that now. You're not playing with small-time crooks, you know; you'll need protection from the police till this gang is smashed, or they'll get you just as surely as they got the others!"

Sam Crawford's hands were clenched so tightly that the whites of his knuckles showed, and his forehead was corrugated in a sullen frown. He was obviously weighing up the pros and cons of his present position and finding it none too happy. There was a heavy silence in the room; everyone seemed to be experiencing a feeling of tension, except Harry Denver who still perched on the edge of the desk with his arms folded.

Sam's breathing became gradually more noticeable until he almost appeared to be gasping for breath. "All right … I'll talk … but I got to have a drink first. I'm all shot to pieces."

His distress was obviously genuine, and Harry looked inquiringly at the other two, for he hadn't a notion where he would get a drink in New Scotland Yard at ten-thirty on a Sunday morning. Then it became obvious that Sam was referring to the small silver flask which had been taken from him when he was searched.

At a nod from Sir Richard, Rymer passed it to Harry, who held on to it for a moment. "First of all, Sam, tell us something about this set-up that's responsible for the jewel robberies."

"I – I don't know much about it … it's run by a bloke who calls himself Grey Moose … he looks after everything."

"How does he get the stuff out of the country?"

"I don't know anything about that – I think it's by aeroplane … a private plane."

"And the airfield?"

"I've never set eyes on it."

"But you've seen Grey Moose? You'd recognise him again?"

Sam gulped hard, appeared to be about to say something, then suddenly grabbed the flask from Harry's hand. For some ten seconds he noisily swallowed down the spirit – and Harry judged the flask to have been well over half full. But almost before he had finished the flask fell from Sam's hands. He sank back in his chair, the blood draining from his face.

"Sam – what is it?"

Sam seemed to be struggling for breath. "I – I – my throat –"

Harry picked up the flask and sniffed it. Mingling with the smell of whisky was the unmistakable odour of carbolic acid. "Where did you get this whisky?" he asked.

Sam's hands were clawing at his throat, then he clutched his stomach, obviously in great pain. "The Kingfisher –" he gasped, rolling forward on the floor.

Bowen knelt and lifted Sam's head whilst Harry felt his purse. Sir Richard picked up the telephone and asked for a police surgeon immediately.

"It's too late," said Harry, looking up a minute later. "He's dead."

"Yes, he's dead all right," repeated Rymer, tonelessly. "What was in that flask, Mr Denver?"

"Whisky, mixed with enough carbolic acid to kill three men, I should imagine," replied Harry. "It might be an idea to send it down to your Fingerprints Department first and have it tested before it goes to the laboratory. There's just a chance there may be some smudges that would give us a clue."

"He said he had it from the Kingfisher," said Rymer.

"That was the whisky. It doesn't necessarily follow that the poison was put in at the same time."

"No, that's true."

"Are you sure it's too late?" asked Sir Richard anxiously. "Perhaps if we could force an antidote …"

"You'd be wasting your time," murmured Harry.

"But it's – it's impossible!" exclaimed the bewildered Sir Richard. This was the first time in his long experience that anything like this had happened inside Scotland Yard and he found it difficult to believe.

"We'd better give him the kiss of life till the doctor gets here," said Bowen, preparing to do so.

But it was obviously too late.

There was suddenly a sharp knock at the door.

"That'll be the doctor now," said McKendrick. "Come in!"

The door opened and the Sergeant from the front hall came in with one of the familiar buff slips filled in by waiting callers. "There's a gentleman to see you, sir," he said to Sir Richard.

"I can't see him now! Tell him to phone!" snapped the Assistant Commissioner.

The Sergeant hesitated, then said diffidently, "He said it was rather important, sir, and he's made a special journey …"

"Oh, hell!" said Sir Richard. "Who is it?"

"It's a Mr Dancey, sir. Mr Benjamin Dancey."

109

CHAPTER TWELVE

"Dancey?" repeated Sir Richard, taking the slip from the Sergeant. "That's the fellow who's staying at the Kingfisher, isn't it?"

"That's right, sir. He's an antiquarian, so he says," replied Bowen.

"H'm … maybe he's stumbled across something."

"He's a cute old bird, sir," put in Harry. "I guess it might be as well to see him."

"All right, Sergeant," nodded Sir Richard. "Ask him to wait a few minutes. I'll phone when I'm free."

The Sergeant withdrew unobtrusively, and they turned to the body of Sam Crawford again.

"Just our confounded luck," groaned Rymer. "In another couple of minutes he'd have told us everything we want to know."

"How did the poison get in the flask?" said Sir Richard, with a bewildered air. "He certainly wasn't the type to commit suicide; I'm sure he didn't know the liquor was poisoned."

"Whoever filled the flask at the Kingfisher could have done it," Harry pointed out. "Or it might have happened any time since, if someone else had access to it."

"You mean it might have been another arranged job – just as they liquidated the night watchman at Gloucester?" suggested Bowen.

"Could be," said Harry.

The arrival of the doctor cut short any further speculation. He lost no time in pronouncing that Sam Crawford was dead and the body was quickly removed to the mortuary. The doctor was also shown the flask, and he asked to be allowed to analyse the dregs as soon as possible. In the meantime it was sent to the Fingerprints Department, who very soon reported back that the only prints upon it of which they had any record were Sam Crawford's.

Left alone with Harry while his assistant attended to the formalities, Sir Richard began brooding over his reports on the Brighton robbery. He seemed in no hurry to send for Mr Dancey and Harry had no intention of leaving until he had done so. He refused one of McKendrick's cigarettes and lit one of his own Chesterfields. Sir Richard went on turning over papers; Harry puffed neat rings of smoke towards the fireplace, and neither spoke for two or three minutes.

Then the Assistant Commissioner said, "This business seems to get more and more involved. Do you think that poison was put in his flask at the Kingfisher, Denver?"

Harry shrugged. "Your guess is as good as mine, Chief. The point is he was rubbed out at just the right moment when he might have been some use to us. I guess we've got to write him off the books and try something else."

"Such as what?"

"Right now, I'm trying to dream up a little scheme," replied Harry as if he did not wish to be interrupted.

Sir Richard relapsed into a moody silence once more and read through a couple of pages. Suddenly he stopped and placed a finger on the paper to keep his place. "There's rather an interesting point here, Denver. I don't know if it means anything …"

"Yes, sir?"

"It seems that a Constable on his beat just before the robbery remembers talking to a girl in a smart sports car, and he's convinced that she had some connection with the affair. She insisted on parking just round the corner, although it was forbidden."

"Then why didn't he move her on?"

"He says she promised she wouldn't be more than a couple of minutes; in fact, he was still arguing with her – so he says – when the lorry came charging down the hill."

"Did he take the number of the car?"

"I'm afraid he didn't get round to that. But there's a fairly detailed description of the girl here." He referred to the report once more, then went on, "Yes – slim – wearing expensive tailor-made suit – fair hair, almost platinum – blue eyes – a set of golf clubs in the back of the car – no jewellery, except a gold ring with a tiny diamond-shaped watch set in it."

"A diamond-shaped watch?" queried Harry sharply, his eyes catching Sir Richard's. "Now, where did I …"

"Yes?" said Sir Richard expectantly.

But Harry shook his head.

"Can you recall seeing some woman wearing one of those ring-watches?"

"I can, but I guess there are hundreds about."

"Who was it?"

"Oh, just a neighbour of mine in the country."

"H'm … well, we've tried to trace the girl, but we haven't had any luck so far, and I'm beginning to doubt whether we will."

"I guess you're right at that," said Harry, frowning thoughtfully as he called to mind the picture of Sally Harrison passing his front gates in her Harman-Grade, with golf clubs in the back … But there must have been dozens of girls in sports cars carrying golf clubs. After all, it was Saturday, and he knew Sally was a fairly regular visitor to the Sevenoaks club. He carefully lighted another cigarette from the butt of its predecessor, which he stubbed out on the ashtray … "Sir Richard," he began with some hesitation, "I've got a kind of idea that might bust this racket open. It's taking a big chance, mind …"

"We've got to take risks, Denver. Things are getting pretty desperate. I had the Home Secretary on the phone last night, hinting there might be questions in the House if we don't put a stop to this business quite soon. So if you've got any sort of an idea, for heaven's sake let's hear it!"

Still Harry hesitated. "It's pretty tricky, Sir Richard. The whole thing would have to be very carefully planned."

"We can settle all that later. What is it you suggest?"

Harry pulled at his cigarette. "There's an old firm of family jewellers just round the corner from Bond Street called Trevelyan's. Heard of them?"

"Of course."

"I once did young Eric Trevelyan a good turn – he'd been having some trouble about a necklace bought by a distinguished member of the peerage whose lady friend professed to take a dislike to it and returned a fake in its place … but that's another story."

"Go on," urged Sir Richard with some impatience.

"Now, supposing it became known that Trevelyan's had a very valuable stone in their safe – the Brailsham Diamond, for instance. It seems to me there's a sporting chance that our friends might be tempted to pay Trevelyan's an unheralded visit – but in this case it wouldn't be entirely unexpected."

McKendrick drummed his fingers on his desk and seemed to be deep in thought.

"We're pretty sure by now," continued Harry, "that these jobs the gang has pulled off have been very carefully planned. Okay then! It's up to us to start planning ahead too."

"Just what do you mean, exactly?"

Harry knocked the ash off his cigarette. "Let's presume that our friends have heard that Trevelyan's have the Brailsham Diamond; what's the first thing they do? They take steps to make quite sure that the report is correct. They'll do that before they make a single move towards planning a

113

robbery." He could see that Sir Richard was becoming interested.

"You mean they'll get somebody to make an inquiry in the ordinary business channels?" McKendrick queried.

"That's it! And that's where my friend Eric Trevelyan comes in. I shall get him to let me have a full list of all inquiries about this stone, and maybe one of them will give us a clue."

Sir Richard stroked his chin as he considered the scheme. It certainly seemed a step towards carrying the war into the enemy's country. During the past weeks he had felt frustrated and baffled at every turn, for there seemed to be no way of anticipating any move from the gelignite gang. There was no knowing where they would strike next, and they covered their tracks so effectively that they had left very few clues. Furthermore, when they had enlisted the help of anyone with a criminal record they had taken good care to eliminate him before he could be made to talk. McKendrick looked at Harry with new respect. "Well, now, let's go into this seriously," he began, settling himself back in his chair. "Is your friend Trevelyan a man to be trusted?"

"Absolutely. What's more, Eric is always game to take a chance. But we've got to play this carefully, Sir Richard. That gang wasn't born yesterday; we haven't got to hand them this on a platter or they'll get scared right away. I reckon a short paragraph in the *Gem Trader* is all that's needed, and Eric will see to that. Of course, I can put it around to one or two contacts of my own – there's Max Hood, for instance. I happen to know he's had his eye on the Brailsham Diamond for at least a couple of years."

"He's the fellow we nearly pinned that receiving charge on in the Curzon Street affair. He got out of the country just an hour too soon and took the stuff with him."

"That's the guy," said Harry cheerfully. "Hood's a pretty smart operator, and he won't suspect anybody of making a tool of him. Not even me!"

"It wants careful handling," temporised Sir Richard, liking the scheme better as it developed, and wondering if he could really trust the man who sat opposite him. It was against all his principles to call in outsiders upon even the most trifling affair, for it was his boast that he had a first-class staff who could deal with any emergency. But he had to face the fact that they had proved unequal to the gelignite gang, and his superiors were becoming impatient for results. Denver's suggestion at least offered some opportunity for positive action.

"All right, Denver," he said at last. "I'll leave this to you for the time being, but keep me informed. And by the by, the fewer people who are let in on this, the better chance it will have of succeeding."

"You've taken the words right out of my mouth, Sir Richard!" said Harry fervently. "I shall only tell when it's absolutely necessary. In fact, I don't see any reason to let anybody in on it, except Eric, until we get an actual tip-off that the gang's interested."

"That's settled then," nodded Sir Richard. "Now, I suppose I'd better see this Mr Dancey. Maybe you should hang on, just in case he's got something that gives us a bearing …"

"Thank you, Sir Richard," said Harry, who had every intention of staying to meet Mr Dancey unless he was bodily thrown out.

Sir Richard picked up the phone and gave the necessary instructions, and presently the dapper little figure, obviously wearing his best suit, with neat wash-leather gloves, appeared in the doorway. In one hand he carried a copy of one of the more literary Sunday newspapers and a small Greek testament with which he had been passing the time in the waiting room.

"Why, Mr Denver!" he exclaimed, recognising Harry at once. "How very pleasant to meet you again in such unique surroundings. This is the first time I've been inside this very remarkable building."

Harry smiled and introduced him to Sir Richard, who courteously asked him to take a seat.

"Would you like a cigarette, Mr Dancey?" asked Harry, opening his silver case and offering it. "Those are Turkish on that side – or I've some American ones in my pocket if you prefer them."

"Turkish!" echoed Mr Dancey, selecting nevertheless a familiar English brand. "A strange country, Mr Denver – Turkey, I mean. A most interesting history. I've made quite a study of their ancient architecture; a fascinating subject. We must have a chat about it some time."

Sir Richard had been looking through the papers in his file and finally selected that which contained Mr Dancey's statement. "Are you still at the Kingfisher Inn, Mr Dancey?"

"Yes, as a matter of fact, I am. I had intended to leave, but I was out for a walk one day this week in the Chevening direction and I came on two young men who were excavating what they assured me was a Roman villa. It was really quite fascinating. I've been there every day since, so I decided to stay on for a while in spite of this deplorable affair."

He was obviously prepared to ramble on in this vein indefinitely, so Sir Richard pulled him up with another abrupt question. "Mr Dancey, why have you come here to see me this morning?"

Dancey sat bolt upright for a moment, looked round the room as if to make sure there were no concealed eavesdroppers, then leaned forward and said confidentially,

"It's about that club room, Sir Richard. I'm getting rather worried …"

"You mean the room where we found that damp patch on the floor?" prompted Harry. "Where the Elks or Rangers meet each week?"

"The Antediluvian Order of Bison," Mr Dancey corrected him in his thin, precise tone. "They meet once a week on a Thursday. I made inquiries about that. The point is, that room is being used on other nights by some other organisation."

"How do you know that?" demanded Sir Richard.

"Because my bedroom happens to be immediately above it, and as is often the case with these old inns the floor and ceiling are one and the same. I can hear voices quite distinctly."

"You mean you can tell what they're saying?"

"No, I can't hear the actual words. But the sound of the voices is loud enough to keep me awake – very annoying, I assure you."

"Then they keep pretty late hours?"

"Their last meeting went on till midnight."

"But it might be a special Committee meeting of these Bisons, or whatever they call themselves," Sir Richard suggested.

Dancey waved the idea aside. "No, no, I'm quite sure it's nothing of the sort," he insisted.

"What makes you so sure of that?" asked Harry with some interest.

"Because I made inquiries of the Secretary, and he assured me that no feminine members are admitted to the Antediluvian Order of Bison," explained Mr Dancey solemnly. "And one of the persons at those conclaves was most certainly a woman!"

CHAPTER THIRTEEN

Mr Dancey proved a tenacious caller. Sir Richard, quite obviously, did not know what to make of him. On the face of it he seemed merely a harmless retired schoolmaster with a passion for antiques and ancient ruins, but one could never be quite sure nowadays, Harry reminded himself yet again. So many apparently respectable people concealed mysterious illicit activities behind an outward appearance of middle-class prosperity. If Mr Dancey were really a staid little ex-dominie would he really wish to stay at the Kingfisher after that distressing evening? There were times when Mr Dancey seemed to display an almost morbid interest in the death of the Superintendent; at others he appeared to regard it as a mere incident in the day's routine.

Although Harry found all this intriguing it was obvious that Sir Richard was rather worried. He checked over Mr Dancey's statement and found no flaw in it. He asked more questions about the mysterious meetings without throwing any fresh light on the matter. Indeed, Mr Dancey's main complaint seemed to be that his sleep had been disturbed which robbed him of his concentrative powers when he wished to investigate the local antiquities the following day. Harry professed to take a serious interest in the Roman villa and urged the little man to stay on at the Kingfisher for a time. It would be useful to know where he was exactly, and if he were in no way involved he would at least prove a thorn in the side of George Bates.

However, the party broke up at last. Mr Dancey promised to keep in touch with Scotland Yard; Harry exchanged a brisk farewell with Sir Richard, saying he would telephone him as soon as he had made "the arrangements". McKendrick nodded understandingly and saw them to the door.

Mr Dancey departed for Charing Cross en route for Bayswater to collect a change of clothing from his flat, and Harry walked round into Charing Cross Road to get a taxi, which took him to the address in Chelsea which Diana had given him.

He arrived soon after one and found her on the fourth floor of a fair-sized block of flats. The sun was filtering through the long window of her comfortably furnished living room, transforming the room into a semblance of those interiors favoured by early Dutch painters.

He sank into one of the armchairs and watched Diana putting finishing touches to the table in an alcove by the window. "You've got yourself fixed up pretty nicely here," he commented, his gaze wandering idly over the books packed tightly into the shelves beside his chair. He was surprised at the remarkable range of subjects they covered. "You're certainly Little Miss Inquire Within," he murmured, picking up a book on the history of South African diamond mining and turning the pages until he came to a brief description of the discovery of the famous Brailsham Diamond. He closed the book and replaced it, then rose and said, "Can I do anything to help? I should have asked."

"That's all right," smiled Diana. "Mrs Bentley will take care of everything … You can pour a drink if you like," she added as an afterthought, indicating a cocktail cabinet near the fireplace.

"That's not a bad idea, either. I feel I've earned a drink this morning. What will it be?"

"Sherry for me, please – the light one."

He poured out the sherry for her and mixed himself a gin and French.

"Has anything special happened this morning?" she inquired as she sipped her drink.

119

He gave her a brief resumé of the poisoning of Sam Crawford, carefully omitting the more gruesome details.

She was not so upset as he had expected. For one thing she had not known Crawford, and for another she could feel little remorse for any member of the gang which she felt convinced was responsible for her brother's death. In fact, the only sign of emotion she betrayed was one of disappointment that Sam had died before he could enlighten them in any way about the gang's activities.

"This would have been a scoop for the evening papers on a weekday," she reflected as they finished their drinks. "I don't suppose a man has ever been poisoned inside Scotland Yard before."

"And I should say it's pretty unlikely ever to happen again," observed Harry. "I guess the morning papers will get the scoop instead. Sir Richard was on the telephone to the Press Bureau just before I left."

"I wonder if I should phone our News Editor, just in case the crime man doesn't get the tip," mused Diana.

"Wait till after lunch," he advised.

"Yes, of course. They won't be on duty until tea-time."

There was a gentle tap on the door, which opened to admit Mrs Bentley, Diana's Scottish housekeeper, carrying a heavily laden tray. She was a plain little woman whose face was completely transformed on the comparatively rare occasions when she permitted herself to smile.

"Ye'd best get on with this while it's hot," she ordered, laying the dishes on the table, for she was firmly convinced that Diana was underfed except when she was at home.

"M'm … this is what I call good home cooking," said Harry, wrinkling his nose appreciatively, thereby making Mrs Bentley his friend for life. "I just can't wait to get started."

When Mrs Bentley had disappeared he said, "You've sure got a treasure out there. I didn't think there were any like that left nowadays."

"What about your Mr Miles?" she smiled.

"Oh, Miles is all right, I guess."

"We'd better not introduce them," said Diana, "or they might marry and leave us in the lurch."

"In that case we'd just have to look after each other. And that might not be such a bad idea," concluded Harry with a speculative gleam in his eye.

Hastily she changed the subject and asked if there was any more news of the Brighton robbery.

Mrs Bentley had brought in the coffee and left them sitting in the comfortable armchairs when she suddenly returned carrying a flat parcel. "It's my memory again, Miss," she apologised in an abject tone. "It came while ye were out yesterday and I put it at the back of my sideboard and forgot all about it. I hope it's nothing urgent."

Diana took the parcel and turned it over. There was no stamp or indication as to who had sent it. "Wasn't there any message, Mrs Bentley?" she asked.

"No, dear. One of those cheeky young errand lads brought it. He just said it was for you and dashed away before I could get in a word. Is it no' something ye've ordered, Miss?"

Diana wrinkled her forehead. "I can't recall asking for anything to be delivered."

"You didn't sign for it, Mrs Bentley?" Harry asked.

"No, sir. The young man was away before I could even turn round."

"Maybe it's a present from an unknown admirer," suggested Harry lightly.

"Well, we'll soon see. Drink your coffee while I open it," she said, dismissing Mrs Bentley, who was obviously a little disappointed.

Diana produced a pair of scissors and snipped the string round the parcel, unfolding the paper and revealing a very ordinary record made by a well known company. She looked inside the sleeve and searched through the outside paper, but there was no sign of any message. "This is all very mysterious," she said.

"*Must* be some unknown admirer – too shy to put a note inside," he declared, sipping his coffee.

Diana looked across at him. "Harry – it wasn't you, was it?"

He shook his head somewhat wistfully. "No, Diana. I'm sorry to say it wasn't. I never seem to get any good ideas like that when I should."

More intrigued than ever, she took the record from its sleeve and examined it. "It's come from someone who knows me pretty well," she announced. "This is my favourite piano piece – Debussy's *Clair de Lune*. It's the very latest recording, too, by that new Hungarian pianist."

"Maybe someone at the office," suggested Harry vaguely, "or even one of your readers."

"Yes, it's possible. I'm simply dying to hear it. I've already worn out three records of this piece."

"Finish your coffee first," said Harry quickly, as she moved towards the large radiogram that stood near the window. He couldn't have told her why he suddenly felt anxious that she should not play the record immediately. However, she did as he suggested, and returned to her chair ro drink her coffee.

When he had finished his own coffee Harry set down his cup on a side table and walked over to the radiogram. "This is a pretty nice little job," he said admiringly. "Looks as if it's a hand-made cabinet."

"Yes, it is. My brother gave it to me for a twenty-first birthday present," she replied, and there was just the barest perceptible catch in her voice.

Harry walked round the radiogram, examining it from every angle, and he was still doing so when Diana rose from her chair, opened the lid, and slipped the disc on to the turntable. She was just about to press the switch when he caught her hand.

"Wait a minute, honey," he said. "I've got a feeling there's a catch in this somewhere."

"A catch in it?" she echoed. "But that's just an ordinary record, what possible harm can there be –"

Nevertheless, he took her arm and gently pushed her back into her chair. "Looks to me like we might be walking right into something with our chins stuck out," he mused. "Whoever sent you this was sure you'd rush to put it on the record-player so as to hear this wonderful new pianist …" He picked up the record and looked at it closely. "This seems to be the genuine article all right, there's nothing sinister about it …" He put it back on the turntable. Then he took a magnifying glass from his waistcoat pocket and looked at the needle in the sound-box. As far as he could see it was quite harmless. "That leaves the record-player itself," he mused. "And whoever sent you that record obviously intended you to play it. By the way, is the radiogram in its usual position?"

She came over to him. "It's been moved a little farther from the wall, I think, but Mrs Bentley might easily have done that when she was dusting." She bent down to look at the front of the cabinet. "This gauze in front of the speaker seems rather more loose than usual," she told him.

"All right," he nodded. "Now you go and sit down over yonder, well out of harm's way."

Having checked the connections at the back of the set and ascertained that it was properly plugged in to the power supply he turned the knob which switched it on and waited for some seconds until he heard a gentle hum. Then, standing well to the side of the cabinet, he lifted the tone arm and swung it over to the turntable.

As he did so there was a loud report and the tone arm jumped out of his hand to grind noisily across the record. A wisp of acrid smoke slowly filtered through the gauze in front of the speaker.

"Harry!" Diana exclaimed, starting from her chair. "Are you all right?"

"Sure, I'm all right." He walked across the room and noted that a bullet had chipped the top of a picture frame and buried itself in the wall. It had obviously had an upward trajectory from a revolver somewhere down inside the speaker and had been fired by the movement of the tone arm.

"Lucky I wasn't standing right in front there, as you'd have done if I'd let you start that record," he told her.

The girl shuddered. "Thank goodness you were here," she said.

He borrowed a screwdriver and removed a section of the radiogram to reveal the revolver neatly clamped in position and connected to the tone arm by an ingenious spring device.

He whistled softly to himself as he worked, then said after a moment, "I don't want to scare you, Diana, but we've got to be pretty careful from now on. This is a warning in more ways than one."

She nodded understandingly. "You mean," she whispered, "that Grey Moose knows my real name?"

CHAPTER FOURTEEN

With a hand that shook slightly Dr Grant depressed the lever of the siphon for a fraction of a second to send the suspicion of a splash of soda into his half-filled tumbler of whisky. By the time he had returned to his armchair he had already taken two large gulps. The doctor was plainly ill at ease.

He settled in his chair and lighted one of the black cheroots to which he was addicted, but even this did not seem to soothe his nerves. Ever since he had received a mysterious telephone call to inform him that the police had picked up Sam Crawford he had been irritable and on edge. This was the first time the Yard had managed to bring in one of the gang alive, and it had him slightly rattled. The mysterious caller had ordered Sally to meet him in the entrance to Charing Cross Underground station at 11a.m., so she had taken her car and left for Town just after ten. Since then Grant had heard nothing.

Though he had combed the Sunday newspaper reports of the Brighton affair there had been no more reference to Sam than the brief intimation that "a man was detained at Purley police station late last night".

It was nearly two o'clock when there was the sound of hastily applied brakes outside, and soon Sally came in. She was obviously not in the best of tempers, peeling off her gloves and throwing them on the settee with an impatient gesture.

"For God's sake give me a drink!" she snapped, and Grant hastened to obey. While he poured it out, she went on, "Has he telephoned?"

"Who?"

"Grey Moose, of course."

He shook his head. "I thought you went to Town specially to see him."

125

She drank nearly half the contents of her glass before replying. "I only know I walked round that blasted Underground station for over two hours," she replied. "There wasn't a sign of him."

Grant looked more worried than ever. "Then you haven't heard anything more about Sam?"

"Not a word. They're still holding him, as far as I know."

Grant emptied his own glass. "I hope to God he doesn't talk," he said with a troubled frown. "I always said he was told a damn sight too much!"

"He had to be told a certain amount," she retorted.

"There was no need for the chief to let him know who he was."

She went to the sideboard and poured another drink. "It's too late to go into that now. Whether he talks or not he'll be taken care of. You can rely on the chief for that, at any rate."

The door opened suddenly and Joe Wilcox came in. His cherubic features were less cheerful than usual; it was obvious that he, too, was somewhat worried. "Any news?" he demanded hoarsely.

"No," replied Grant abruptly." And I've told you not to come here in broad daylight! We don't want to attract any more attention than we can help, with those plain-clothes men still hanging about the village."

"I came the back way," said Joe. "Not a soul set eyes on me. This place is quiet as the grave on a Sunday – fair gives me the jitters. Mind if I have a drink?"

"Help yourself," said Grant shortly.

Joe poured himself a generous measure of rum. "You got the stuff out all right?" he asked Sally.

"As far as I know," she replied somewhat distantly. "It went off right on schedule."

Joe heaved a sigh of relief. "That's all right then. If only that damn fool Sam hadn't let them get him this job would've been plain sailing right from start to finish. As sweet a little job as ever I was mixed up in." He fumbled in his pockets for a cigarette and lit it. "Doc," he went on cautiously, "do you think Sam will tell 'em anything?"

"Oh, shut up!" Sally said fiercely. Her nerves were plainly on edge.

Joe looked from one to the other apprehensively. "What's the matter?" he asked. "There's nothin' gone wrong, has there?"

"We don't know – we haven't heard anything," replied Grant.

Joe immediately began to look troubled again. "Supposin' … supposin' they get it out of him who Grey Moose is," he breathed. "I reckon that'd just about bust the whole set-up. They'd hunt us down like rats in a hole –"

"Will you be quiet!" cried Sally, her eyes blazing. "They'll never get the chief … never!"

"Maybe not," sniffed Joe. "I dare say 'e's got 'is plans made for doing a bunk. We ain't all of us as lucky!"

"Oh, pull yourselves together," said Grant abruptly. "Things aren't as bad as that yet by a long way. Whatever they get out of Sam they'll only have his word for it. They'll never get any real proof."

This seemed to cheer Joe a little. "Yes, and what's more they won't find it easy to make Sam talk," he affirmed. "That boy knows how to keep his mouth shut!" He was about to enlarge on this when the telephone rang.

"I'll take it in the study," said Sally quickly, going out of the room.

"That'll be him, I reckon," nodded Joe. "And about time too, if you ask me."

"Nobody is asking you anything at the moment," said the doctor restlessly. "Better have another drink and say as little as possible."

127

So the two men lapsed into a moody silence that was unbroken for nearly five minutes, until the door handle turned and Sally came back. For perhaps five seconds they looked at her without speaking.

Then she said quietly, "That was the chief."

"Well?" asked Grant, moistening his lips.

"Sam Crawford's dead," she announced in what was almost a casual tone.

"Good God!" exclaimed Grant. "How did it happen?"

She shrugged her elegant shoulders. "He was just about to talk … but Grey Moose got him in time."

"Was that why he didn't meet you?" inquired Grant.

"He didn't say. There were so many other things to discuss."

"Such as?"

She walked across the room and sat in a straight-backed chair beside the table. "Joe, have you ever heard of Trevelyan's, the jewellers just off Bond Street?" she asked.

"Yes, of course I 'ave. I was in a smash-and-grab job there a few years ago. Real swindle it turned out to be – the ruddy commissionaire got in the way and we 'ad to make a run for it empty-'anded."

"Well, this time there won't be any slip-ups like that," she assured him.

"You mean the chief's planning a new job already?" Grant inquired.

"Yes, and you'll never guess where the tip came from?"

"Where?"

"Duke Leroy got it from our old friend, Mr Denver! On the phone. Of course, he gave the wire to the chief the minute he heard."

"Is it something special then?" asked Grant.

"I'll say it is! Lord Brailsham's family estate are putting the Brailsham Diamond on the market at last – and it'll be on view at Trevelyan's!"

Joe whistled softly to himself. "That'll be worth a packet! Best part of twenty thousand, or more, I shouldn't wonder." He paused for a moment, then said, "How the 'ell does Denver get to 'ear these things?"

"You know Harry," said Sally. "He's got his nose in everybody's business. Leroy says he's after that diamond, and the chief has other plans."

Grant looked up suspiciously. "Are you quite sure of this?"

"The chief was in no doubt about it on the phone."

Grant seemed frankly incredulous. "After all we've heard about Harry Denver –"

"It's that girl," put in Sally curtly. "I've seen him around with her. Leroy says Harry's fallen for her. He needs more money to create an impression."

"More likely it's those blasted cards I 'ave to leave around," snorted Joe. "I always said that was a ruddy silly idea."

Sally swung round on him. "You're paid damn well to do as you're told!" she flared. "You haven't done so badly out of it so far."

Muttering to himself Joe went over to the sideboard and poured himself another drink.

"The chief is quite certain about Denver and this girl?" asked Grant.

"Of course."

"Then why is he acting on his tip?"

"The chief is more than a match for Harry Denver, whatever he may be up to," retorted Sally. "Besides, the tip was to Duke Leroy, not the chief."

"I see. Anything else?"

"Yes, Grey Moose sent a special message to you. He says Harry Denver has got to be taken care of. Can you handle it?"

Dr Grant laughed mirthlessly. "Leave Mr Denver to me!"

CHAPTER FIFTEEN

Standing just round the corner from Bond Street, the old-fashioned family firm of Trevelyan's specialised in antique jewellery. They had their own exclusive clientele, and bought up the heirlooms of many an impoverished county family.

Jonathan Trevelyan was a keen business man, but he appreciated the policy of paying a fair price that left him a reasonable profit and a satisfied customer who would recommend him to other profitable clients.

Eric did not approve of all his father's ultra-scrupulous transactions, nor indeed of some of his cautious business methods. He often complained that a shop of their repute should have a turnover of at least three times its present figure, but the older man would rebuke him sharply and tell him that all too few people left in the world concentrated upon quality nowadays, and Trevelyan's had a duty towards their blue-blooded customers which must never be allowed to take second place to any get-rich-quick policy.

On the Thursday after the Brighton robbery Eric rang up Harry Denver just before lunch and said, "About that little matter … could we meet some time fairly soon?"

"Okay – see you this evening," replied Harry promptly. "Not at the shop, though. Is there anywhere near where we can talk?"

"There's my club –"

"No use – I want to bring a girl friend along, if you've no objection."

"None at all. I'll see you at the Vine, then – it's the little pub in the next turning to ours, as you come from Piccadilly."

"I'll find it," promised Harry. "Six o'clock be okay?"

"That'll do nicely."

Harry replaced his receiver, then picked it up again to telephone Diana's office. She had not seen him for three days, but he had been telephoning her twice a day during the week to make sure she was all right.

He arranged to call for her at the office that evening and was waiting in the main hall promptly at five-thirty. A taxi dropped them outside the Vine just after six o'clock, and they found Eric Trevelyan lounging against the bar counter in the lounge. Noting with some satisfaction that the room was otherwise empty, apart from the barman, Harry quickly introduced Diana and Eric, and they carried their drinks over to a distant corner.

"I had the devil's own job talking the old man into this little stunt of yours," Eric confided as they sat down. "At first I thought I wouldn't say anything to him, but I knew it would come round to him in the end; then there'd be a real balloon ascent!"

Diana rather liked the look of Eric. He was a sturdy young man with friendly eyes and a forthright manner and when he smiled he displayed a perfect set of teeth which were white enough for a toothpaste advertisement.

"I'm sorry if I've upset the old man," said Harry.

"That's perfectly all right, old boy. He hasn't forgotten the good turn you did me last year, and as soon as I mentioned your name he gave us his blessing!" Eric laughed again and buried his nose in his tankard. Presently, he set it down and delicately mopped his mouth with a large silk handkerchief. "Well, we've certainly had some inquiries about the Brailsham Diamond," he announced. "I had them all referred to me personally, as you suggested, and it's kept me pretty busy, I can tell you. Most of the inquiries came from people in the trade. In fact, so far there have been only three outside people. One of them was Lady Tollitt, an old client who makes it her business to nose into everything, though she hardly ever buys anything. Then there was a man we didn't know who said he was a jeweller in Salisbury and thought he might have a client for the stone. We checked up on him, and he's genuine."

"And the third?" queried Harry softly.

"The third was a girl …"

"Ah –" murmured Harry, his face alight with interest.

"She came in this morning and asked to see some filigree silver brooches, and she actually bought one. Then, just before she left she asked me if it was true we had the Brailsham Diamond and could she possibly take a peep at it?"

"Go on," said Harry.

"I tipped off the commissionaire and gave the nod to a couple of the men behind the counter. Then I fetched it for her from the safe. I felt a bit jittery at first, but I didn't see how a girl on her own like that could possible hope to get away with anything."

"And did she?" demanded Diana eagerly.

"No, of course not. She just took a pretty close look at the stone and admired it. Then she wished me good morning."

Harry broke open a packet of Chesterfields and passed them round. "What was she like?" he asked.

Eric's eyes glittered for a fleeting moment.

"Distinctly voluptuous type," he declared appreciatively. "Dazzling blonde – all the dangerous curves in exactly the right places – in fact, a real dish!"

"Yes, but don't you remember anything more definite? That description might fit any showgirl from the Palladium," Harry protested.

"Was she wearing anything special?" prompted Diana.

"Let's see now … she had a mink cape … and – and good heavens, yes! I remember now. She wore one of those diamond-shaped watches set in a ring. They're a French line – I begged the old man to handle them, but he looked right down his nose."

"You're quite sure about that watch?" persisted Harry.

"Quite sure, because we once considered …" He suddenly stopped short and looked across at Harry. "I say, do you think you know this girl?"

"I guess maybe I do," replied Harry casually. "The point is, Eric, would you recognise her again if I asked you to identify her some time?"

"You can bet your last dollar on that, Harry!" grinned Eric Trevelyan. "I'd know her in a million. She's got style … she's got that little bit extra … she's got …"

"Have a drink, Eric," smiled Harry, signalling to the barman.

***

"You really knew that girl?" asked Diana ten minutes later as they walked towards Harry's favourite restaurant.

"Didn't you?" he temporised.

"Well, yes, it sounded rather like that girl we saw at the night-club – your neighbour …"

"Sally Harrison. I noticed that ring with a watch in it when she and her uncle had dinner with me. It is rather unusual – even that officer at Brighton remembered it."

He said no more until they were seated in the restaurant and had given their order. Then he said slowly, "I guess it's high time we dropped in on Dr Grant and his charming niece. There's one or two things they might help us to sort out."

"No time like the present," nodded Diana.

He regarded her with a slight frown. "I guess you shouldn't get mixed up in this – just in case."

"We'll go down immediately after dinner," she announced.

"Yes, but Diana, I'm not too sure about this guy, Grant …"

"All the more reason you should have a witness," said Diana.

"I dare say, but I've a hunch this might be dangerous ..."

"Are you trying to stand me up, Harry?"

They looked at each other for a moment and laughed.

CHAPTER SIXTEEN

Lew Paskin was not his real name, but he used it more than any of his other aliases, and was widely known by it from Hoxton to Wapping Stairs.

At the moment Lew was on to one of the cushiest berths he had come across for many a day. Nominally he was in charge of the household at White Towers, Caldicott Green, but he was not really expected to concern himself with domestic chores, unless he felt like polishing a few spoons to pass the time.

Two women came in every day from the village, and Lew's main job was to keep an eye on them to see they didn't accidentally find or overhear anything that did not concern them. He also had to keep a sharp look-out for strangers. This was the pleasantest occupation Lew had struck since, by some fluke, he had found himself working in the prison library at Wandsworth. But this job at White Towers was much better paid; he was getting fifteen quid a week with a promise of more to come if he was cut in on any of the jobs planned for the future.

Lew was a gaunt specimen and resembled a seedy manservant who had seen better days. Now that his hair had grown again he no longer conformed to the popular conception of the appearance of a hardened criminal.

Harry and Diana had rung the front door bell of White Towers twice before they heard Lew slowly and ponderously drawing back the top and bottom bolts.

"It's a bit early in the evening for all this barricading," Diana whispered, and Harry pressed her arm reassuringly.

Presently the door opened about a foot and the gaunt feature of Lew Paskin surveyed them suspiciously. "Good evening, sir," he said quietly.

"Oh, good evening," smiled Harry. "You remember me – er –"

"Paskin's the name, sir."

"I rather wanted to see Dr Grant," continued Harry pleasantly.

"I'm afraid he's out, sir. He went into Sevenoaks an hour ago."

"Oh, I see." Harry considered this for a moment, then said, "Well, perhaps Miss Harrison –"

"She's with the doctor, sir," interposed Paskin. He spoke in a noncommittal tone, but something told Harry that he was not speaking the truth. "Was the doctor expecting you, sir?" continued Paskin.

Harry shook his head. "Not to my knowledge. But if he's only gone into Sevenoaks maybe we could wait for him?"

Paskin did not seem to welcome this proposal and made no attempt to open the door any wider. "I'm not expecting the doctor back for some time," he announced.

"That's too bad," murmured Harry. "All the same, this matter's rather important – I think we'll wait, if you don't mind."

Lew Paskin hesitated. He knew Harry was a near neighbour and might be calling upon some purely local matter, and the doctor had been very emphatic that the suspicions of the village folk must not be in any way aroused. After an appreciable pause Paskin slowly opened the front door to admit the visitors.

He led the way through the parquet-covered hall into the drawing room, which was expensively furnished and seemed to be in frequent use. There was a small stack of magazines including one or two of a highly technical scientific nature and of American origin. There were also several small-sized reproductions of classical statues.

Paskin waited for them to sit down, then lingered for quite an appreciable time before he moved to the door, as if he could not be certain as to whether he should leave them alone in the room. However at last the door closed quietly behind him, and Diana heaved a tiny sigh of relief.

"Thank goodness he's gone," she said in a low voice. "He certainly gives me the creeps – I don't know what you think of him."

"I guess there are plenty worse types in Hollywood," grinned Harry.

"Strangely enough, that doesn't reassure me very much," replied Diana. "Anyhow, this is quite a swell place – just look at that lovely Persian rug. It must have cost a small fortune."

Harry, who knew little about such things, nodded absently, for his thoughts were busy elsewhere. His roving eye took in the solid oak panels around the wall, the ornately figured ceiling, the wide bay window overlooking a similar view to the one from the back of his own house. He got up and began to walk round slowly, eventually pausing in front of the impressive Adam fireplace, and looking into the empty grate.

Presently he stooped to pick up a cigarette end which had caught his attention. It was still smouldering. "It doesn't look as if the guy who let us in was on the level when he said Miss Harrison had gone with the doctor an hour ago," he mused.

Diana joined him and glanced at the cigarette end. "Of course, it could have been the butler enjoying a quiet little smoke in the best room while the boss is away," she suggested.

Harry waved aside the idea. "I didn't notice he used orange lipstick, did you?"

Diana had to agree that the owner of the cigarette had almost certainly been a woman.

Harry flung the stub back into the grate and stood for some moments with his head leaning against the wide mantelpiece.

Meanwhile Diana was examining a statue of Apollo which stood in a small niche in the same wall as the fireplace. It was about eighteen inches high and fitted so neatly into the recess that they might have been made for each other. Her exceptionally keen eyesight noticed an almost invisible crack which seemed to divide the upper part of the torso from the lower. Intrigued, she touched the top half of the statue with one hand and twisted it gently. It moved fairly easily.

"Harry, come and look at this!"

Roused from his own thoughts, Harry crossed towards Diana and watched as she touched the statue again.

"It's quite loose," she told him and, gripping it more tightly, turned it slowly through an angle of ninety degrees …

As she did so an adjacent section of the oak panelling of the wall nearby began to slide back with a soft grating noise. Harry swung round and peered into the aperture. Then, after glancing quickly at the door and windows to make sure they were not overlooked, he returned to the opening in the wall and tried to see what was on the other side.

"Shall I close it again?" whispered Diana, fearful that someone would come in.

"Not on your life!" he replied, feeling in his pocket and producing a pencil torch.

The narrow beam pierced the gloom beyond the opening, but all he could see when he thrust his head through the small aperture were four bare walls comprising a small room about six feet square.

Diana waited impatiently for him to withdraw his head and shoulders, meanwhile watching the door apprehensively. "Can you see anything?" she whispered urgently.

Harry turned and put out his torch. "It's just a small empty room," he told her. "Rather like one of those old-fashioned clothes cupboards, only larger. All the same, there must be more to it than that or there wouldn't be all this mysterious business with the statue. I'm going inside to look at it more closely."

He managed to pull back the panel another inch or two and began to wriggle his way through it.

"I'm coming too!" declared Diana, still fearful that the manservant might return at any moment.

When Harry was inside he held out his hand and she put one foot cautiously through the opening. It was about eighteen inches above floor level. She had to stoop a little, but she was through the panel much more quickly than her companion. He switched on the torch again and they stood looking round somewhat uncertainly.

"Not very startling, eh?" he said quietly.

Diana noticed that the walls were panelled with the same oak as the drawing room and there was a tiled floor. Set in the middle of the ceiling was a thick glass panel which betokened an electric light but there was no switch visible.

He guessed what she was thinking and said, "Maybe if we close the door that will operate the switch."

Placing her palm against the sliding panel she found that it closed quite easily, and almost at once a soft glow illuminated the tiny room. Even so, it seemed just as bare as ever, without any furniture or ornament.

Then they were suddenly conscious of a slight vibration and the distant hum of a dynamo. Feeling that something was amiss Diana tried to force back the panel, only to discover that it would not budge.

"Here, let me try," Harry said, moving over to her. But the panel would not yield, and it was not easy to get any kind of personal grip upon the smooth woodwork.

140

"Harry!" gasped Diana. "*This room is moving!*"

He looked round anxiously, trying to discover exactly what was happening. A few seconds later it dawned on him.

"It's a lift of some sort!" he told her. "For God's sake keep still …"

It was moving so slowly that it took a little time to make certain in which direction they were going. He knelt on the floor and placed his ear against the wall. The vibration seemed to grow more intense.

"We're going down … I'm sure we're going down!" cried Diana.

He gripped her arm. "It's all right; we're only moving very slowly," he assured her.

They could distinctly feel a very slight sinking movement now. It went on for about a minute, but they would both have sworn it lasted at least half an hour. Then there was a barely noticeable jerk and the vibration ceased.

"Here we are then, sound in wind and limb," said Harry, trying to sound light-hearted.

Diana looked over his shoulder and clutched his arm. He turned his head sharply to see what had caught her eye.

"Harry – look!"

Released by some hidden spring, the panel was slowly sliding open …

CHAPTER SEVENTEEN

Harry Denver's fingers closed over the automatic in his coat pocket. He had been carrying it around for the past week. But there was no sign or sound of any other person outside the lift. When the panel opened the light had automatically switched off, so he produced his torch and, holding it at arm's length, shone it through the aperture.

They seemed to be in a passage which disappeared into the darkness ahead. The chalky walls reflected the light from his torch, and there was a dank, clammy smell that was chilling and depressing. Diana shivered as she followed Harry out of the lift.

The tunnel proved to be about three feet wide and there was a single line of crude flagstones on the floor. Moisture ran down the shiny walls and dripped from the low roof.

"I've got to find out where it leads," he told her in a subdued voice. "Are you coming with me?"

"I'm certainly not staying here!" she replied emphatically, and motioned to him to lead the way.

There was no room for them to walk abreast, even if they had wished to do so, and Harry went on ahead, clicking down the safety catch of his revolver as he moved off.

The stone floor stretched ahead of them as far as they could see. At times the flags were uneven and a little slippery. But they moved along at a reasonable pace, though Harry hesitated from time to time and flashed his torch a little farther ahead.

"This tunnel seems to be pretty old," he muttered. "I've often heard rumours of such things, though they're usually between the monastery and the convent!"

"You've been reading too many guide books," she smiled.

"Anyhow, this would delight Mr Dancey's heart if he knew about it. Excavations are right up his street."

"Perhaps he doesn't know about it," she suggested lightly.

The idea struck Harry with some force. "Yeah … that little guy's always nosing around … maybe he knows more than we think …"

"Perhaps we'll find him down here, looking for fossils or something," she could not resist adding.

When they had gone another twenty yards or so Harry stopped and began to fumble in his waistcoat pocket. He often carried a miniature compass around with him, and he hoped it was in this particular suit. His luck was in. He produced the compass, showed it to Diana, then stood frowning over it for three or four minutes while he tried to get their bearings.

At last he said, "I make it that we're heading in a dead straight line towards the Kingfisher."

"Then at least we'll get a drink at the end of our journey," she laughed.

After a few more yards he got the impression that the tunnel was rising slightly, and a little farther on this became more pronounced.

Looking ahead over Harry's shoulders Diana suddenly caught sight of a faint glimmer of light. "Put the torch out!" she hissed in a tense whisper, and he obeyed immediately. "Can you see that light?" she asked.

He peered ahead and could just discern the dim glow from what seemed to be a small oil lamp. "We must be getting near," he said softly. "The Kingfisher is just about a hundred yards from White Towers in a direct line, and we've come just about that far, I'd say. I'm going to keep the torch switched off, in case there's anyone about near that lamp."

They had to move rather more cautiously now, for the flagstones were becoming more uneven. Presently, moving very carefully indeed, they reached the lamp, which stood on a small ledge about four feet high and six inches wide. It was a small hand-lamp and had been turned fairly low with the

143

result that there was a pungent smell of paraffin. The glass container was almost full so it could not have been burning for very long.

Diana drew up alongside Harry and silently indicated a flight of wooden steps about three feet away.

"We're right under the inn," breathed Harry, and they moved over to the foot of the steps.

Almost immediately they heard a distant murmur of voices. Harry pulled Diana back, flat against the wall, and both stood motionless for a couple of minutes.

The voices continued. Once they heard the sound of a woman talking rapidly, then the men droned on …

"I'm going up the stairs," Harry whispered at length.

"Me, too," she said, clasping the crude wooden handrail that ran up one side of the steps.

They trod cautiously, a step at a time, and the voices from above became gradually more distinct. Then Diana took a step which caused the stair to creak like the crack of a whip. They held their breath and waited for some seconds. But the voice murmured on.

Keeping well to the side nearest the rail they eventually reached the top and could discern the dim outline of a door. Harry realised they were looking through an opening at the back of the cupboard – the cupboard he had seen in the club room on the night Falconer had been murdered. It confirmed his theory that the gang was using that club room for their meetings.

At first they had some difficulty in catching what the people in the room were saying, for a long robe was partly draped in front of the open panel at the back of the cupboard and he was afraid to move it aside. But presently the voices became clearer and he could even recognise them as belonging to George Bates, the innkeeper, Dr Grant, and Sally

144

Harrison. They had flared up in disagreement and the voices were raised accordingly.

"What really happened to Sam – that's what I want to know?" demanded George Bates indignantly.

"Don't be a damned fool!" Sally snapped. "You read the papers, the same as the rest of us."

"Yes, I know. But they're hushing somethin' up. I got to know what really happened."

"All right, George," came the sardonic tones of Dr Grant. "If you really want it straight, Sam had to be – taken care of. He was liable to talk."

There was a momentary pause while George Bates digested the information. Then he demanded hoarsely, "You mean it was – Grey Moose what done it?"

"He was killed, my dear Bates, by drinking from a flask, the contents of which were highly lethal. As to how the poison got inside the flask, the police can't quite decide. They might even ask you some questions about it."

Again there was a pause. Then the sound of George Bates' voice, very subdued. "I – I *did* fill his flask just before the Brighton job. But it was only Scotch whisky … I didn't put nothin' else in …"

"We'll take your word for it," came the sauve tones of Grant. "Let's hope the police will do the same."

"Now look 'ere!" began Bates angrily. "Why the 'ell should I want to poison Sam? He's always been a pal of mine."

"I'm not disputing that," replied Grant equably. "I'm only warning you that the police might ask awkward questions, so mind what you tell them."

"Never mind about that," retorted the landlord. "What I want to know is why Sam 'ad to be taken care of like that?"

"Because," explained Grant patiently, "the police suspected him. He might have talked."

145

"Who says so? How do we know he'd 'ave talked. The papers only said the police 'ad picked him up for questioning. I'll bet Sam wouldn't 'ave told them a thing!"

Harry thought George Bates sounded as if he had been drinking. His voice was thicker than usual, and the note of defiance in it obviously owed something to an external source of stimulation.

"Never mind all that," said the doctor testily. "You're quite aware that we never take any unnecessary chances of that sort."

"That's all very well, but you told us the same tale about the driver at Preston and the watchman at Gloucester. They did the blooming dirty work and then they was just wiped out!"

"You know quite well the Preston man was a bungler who didn't even trouble to wear gloves on the job. We couldn't leave him in circulation with his fingerprints already in the files."

"And the night watchman?"

"I'll admit that was my fault. I gave the poor devil too large a dose of chloroform."

There was silence for a few moments. Harry felt Diana's hand near his and gripped it tightly.

Then they heard George Bates say, only slightly less belligerently, "Well, I dare say it sounds all right. But this Grey Moose cove is a sight too smart for my liking."

"So you think Grey Moose is too smart?" It was a woman's voice speaking now, and Harry immediately identified Sally Harrison as its owner. "It's a lucky thing for all of us he's as smart as he's been these last few months. Otherwise, we should all be several thousand pounds worse off."

"That's very true, my friend," confirmed the grim tones of Dr Grant. "Now, let's stop all this argument and get on with what we're here for."

"Which is what?" inquired yet another voice, which Harry did not recognise.

"If you'll give me a little time I'll explain everything," Grant retorted acidly. "A few days ago Grey Moose got the tip that the Brailsham Diamond was in the possession of Trevelyan's, the Mayfair jewellers. Sally's been round there and taken a look at it, and it's the genuine article all right."

"It's too soon to pull another job right away," objected the strange voice. "We've been takin' too many chances as it is."

"If you'll allow me to finish what I was saying …" continued the doctor bitingly, and the other man subsided. "Soon after Sally had been to Trevelyan's the chief telephoned to say that the Brailsham Diamond was a trap, and if it hadn't been for him we should have stuck our necks right into it."

"Strewth!" ejaculated the landlord, and there was an impressive silence for a few seconds.

Then the strange voice asked, "What about Sally? How do we know she wasn't spotted?"

"Don't worry," said the girl. "I wasn't the only one who inspected that stone. The man in the shop said there'd been twenty or thirty to see it."

"All the same," said Grant, "you'd better lie low for a while. The chief insisted on it."

"Yes, we don't want to run into trouble so soon after the Brighton job," said George Bates. "I wonder whose idea it was to plant that rock."

"You can take it from me that it was Mr Harry Denver's scheme," said the doctor menacingly. "And you may rest assured that Mr Denver's originality will be recognised – all in good time."

147

"'Ere, we don't want no fancy tricks, Doc," said Bates with a note of alarm in his voice. "Like that time you used the air bubbles …"

"You leave it to me," Grant reprimanded. "I can handle these things."

Harry felt Diana give a tiny shudder and he squeezed her hand reassuringly.

"Well, I don't want any more murders around my place," said Bates apprehensively.

"You can rest assured you won't be involved," Grant assured him. "Now, the chief's got another idea up his sleeve, and it's going to be one of the biggest jobs we've tackled so far. He wants you all here on Saturday at ten sharp."

"Is he coming down himself?" asked the landlord.

"He'll be here. And he'll have the proceeds of the Brighton job. The stuff fetches a high price, so I hope everybody will be satisfied."

At this point there were signs that the meeting was breaking up, so Harry motioned to Diana to descend the stairs quickly.

They made very little noise, and when they had reached the bottom there was no sign of anyone following them. They hastened along the passage as fast as they could go, Diana almost slipping on the slimy flagstones. Harry caught her arm just in time. After a while he judged it safe to switch on his torch as there was less chance of their being seen from behind, and after what seemed an age to them in their anxiety they reached the lift.

It was just as they had left it. Diana hurried in first and Harry scrambled in after her. He had no difficulty in closing the panel and the light came on immediately. Once again they heard the hum of the electric motor, and after a few moments they could feel the lift moving slowly upwards.

"It's working all right," said Diana somewhat nervously.

148

"I hope the gent upstairs hasn't been in to see how we were getting on," Harry said, equally nervously.

At last the lift stopped and the panel slid open. They glanced cautiously out into the room beyond, which was quite empty. With any luck their absence would have passed unnoticed. Wasting no time, Harry helped Diana out of the lift and twisted the statue to close the panel. With a sigh of relief they watched it slide gently back into position.

"I guess that's a weight off my mind," he observed. "Now, it might lead to a little unpleasantness if they found us here when they got back, so we'd better get going."

He pressed the bell at the side of the fireplace and shortly they heard footsteps in the hall.

When Lew Paskin reappeared Harry said with an air of an impatient caller, "I'm afraid we can't wait for Dr Grant any longer. Perhaps you'll let him know I called. Maybe I can fix up to see him tomorrow."

"I'll tell the doctor," replied Paskin, holding the door open for them and ushering them out into the hall. He wished them good night and they heard the front door close behind them, followed by a slamming of bolts.

Harry and Diana stood for a moment taking in deep breaths of the fresh night air. They found it hard to realise that they had crammed so much excitement into the past hour or so. Then they walked slowly over to the car.

"Things certainly went our way that time," mused Harry as he pressed the self-starter. "Though I guess it's about time we had a break."

The engine roared into life, he slid into gear, and they moved off.

"Have you time for a bite of supper at my place?" he asked her.

She glanced at her wristwatch and nodded.

149

"Good," he said. "Then we can have a little talk and I'll drive you back to Town afterwards."

Miles opened the door for them and seemed in no way perturbed by the unexpected guest. Within fifteen minutes he had produced a tray of sandwiches and Harry's favourite coffee.

"Diana," Harry said presently, "I'm getting awfully worried about you."

She looked across at him. "I was just about to say the same about you," she confessed. "I couldn't help hearing what Dr Grant said about – 'taking care of you', I think the expression was."

"Oh, I've handled plenty tougher customers than Grant," he assured her. "But I don't want you to be mixed up in this affair. It's too tough for a nice girl like you."

She reached over and squeezed his elbow, "I've tackled some ticklish assignments in my journalistic career," she told him. "I've written up everything from the smuggling racket in the South African diamond mines to night life in Marseilles, so I know a few things about human nature!"

But Harry refused to be pacified. "That's all very well, but these people stop at nothing; you've already seen that. You've got to be on the look-out every minute of the day, unless …"

"Unless what?"

He fidgeted uneasily. "I was wondering if you couldn't take a little holiday. Say a fortnight in Switzerland or the South of France. I reckon you could write your column just as easy from there."

"I don't doubt that I could, but I haven't the slightest intention of going away just yet."

Harry drained his cup and reached for a cigarette. "I can't for the life of me see why you want to be mixed up in this," he said.

"Then I'll tell you," she said firmly, locking her hands over her knees and looking him full in the eyes. "I intend to be mixed up in it because it is my affair as much, or more than, anybody else's. Have you forgotten that Carl Kranston killed my brother?"

"I know, honey, I know," said Harry soothingly. "But why throw yourself into danger as well?" There was a note of pleading in his tone.

"It goes much deeper than that," she told him. "Right from the start of those robberies in Cape Town I had the feeling that sooner or later I should be face to face with Carl Kranston. I can't keep running away from him."

"And what happens when you do meet?" he inquired. "How do you think you'd handle him?"

She reached for her handbag, opened it, and took out a neat little .22 Redvers automatic. "I haven't shown you this before," she said, "but I've been carrying it around with me since David was killed."

"Sure, that's all very well," nodded Harry. "The point is, can you use it?"

"I've been a member of a shooting club ever since I landed here. I know it's only a toy pistol, but I can use it lethally at any distance up to fifteen yards. So you see, you can't get rid of me as easily as that!"

"I don't want to get rid of you," Harry said fervently. "I simply want to keep you out of harm's way."

"Well, it's very sweet of you, Harry, but I'm afraid you've picked on a tough baby this time."

Harry could not repress a grin, but he was obviously still worried.

Diana poured him some more coffee. "At any rate, we know just how wise to us they really are," she consoled him. "What's more, we're certain now that Dr Grant and his girl

151

friend, not to mention that landlord, are in it up to the eyes. All we have to do now is close in on Grey Moose."

"Yes, I'll see Sir Richard first thing in the morning," he decided.

"And what will you suggest?"

"Isn't that obvious?" he said seriously. "The Kingfisher will have to be raided on Saturday evening at all costs."

CHAPTER EIGHTEEN

The following morning, as he drove along the country lanes, Harry speculated idly on how the Brailsham Diamond "plant" had leaked out. As far as he knew, the only people in the secret were high officials at Scotland Yard, Eric Trevelyan, Diana, and himself.

Where had the leak occurred? Could anyone have overheard their conversation with Eric Trevelyan in that little pub off Bond Street? He had already telephoned Eric to ask if he had mentioned the matter to anyone else, only to receive a fervent assurance that, apart from his father, he had not. Asked if his father might have let slip a careless word, Eric had insisted that the old man had been too scared about the whole affair to breathe a syllable to a soul. It seemed that Grey Moose had an able informant who knew how to keep himself well hidden. Could they possibly keep the raid on the Kingfisher a secret?

Parking his car just off the Embankment Harry walked past the Receiver's Office and the Administrative section until he came to the comparatively new C.I.D. building.

As he had previously telephoned to make an appointment, he was admitted to Sir Richard's room almost immediately, and he found the Assistant Commissioner looking just as worried as previously, with a varied assortment of files, letters, and documents in front of him. He welcomed Harry as if he were glad to get a few minutes' relief from the concentration of his desk work. Sir Richard also realised by now that if Harry Denver made an appointment to see him it would most certainly concern some new development that would call for his full attention.

Harry lost no time in rapidly detailing his adventure of the previous evening. Sir Richard was plainly taken aback by the news that their carefully laid trap baited with the Brailsham

153

Diamond had so soon been sprung. For over ten minutes they discussed how this could possibly have come about, but arrived no nearer a solution.

"I don't know what to make of that secret passage," said Sir Richard. "You don't think it's been made recently, do you, Denver?"

"No, sir. It's been there for many a long year, I guess. Some sort of smugglers' set-up between the old inn and the Squire's house maybe. You know more about these fine old English traditions than I do."

"H'm!" grunted the Assistant Commissioner. "I wonder whether the fellow Dancey knows anything about it. He's supposed to be an expert in such things."

"Well, he's staying at the inn, and he had a good look round that club room on the night of the murder," said Harry thoughtfully.

"Are you quite certain he wasn't there last night?"

"If he was, he didn't say a word," replied Harry. "There was some guy there whose voice I didn't recognise, but it wasn't Mr Benjamin Dancey."

"You don't think Dancey could have got wise to anything about the Brailsham Diamond last time he was here? There's just a chance he might have overheard some remark as he came in or left this room. In that case –"

"Dancey would be the man we're after," Harry agreed. "But I'm afraid it isn't as simple as that, Sir Richard."

Sir Richard stroked his chin thoughtfully. "No," he said with some reluctance, "I'm inclined to agree with you. All the same, there's something a bit peculiar about this fellow Dancey."

"He's certainly worth watching," said Harry. "But I've a feeling that the man we're after is a bit nearer home than that."

"Home?" queried the Assistant Commissioner, raising his eyebrows. "You don't mean *here*?"

Harry shrugged. "It's up to you, Sir Richard. I'm only reminding you of the facts. That Brailsham Diamond business was known to Miss Stone, the two Trevelyans, myself – and a bunch of high-ups here at the Yard. You can take your choice. Maybe you think I'm playing in with this gang; in that case I shall just have to try to handle this job on my own …"

"No, no," interposed McKendrick anxiously. "You've been a tremendous help, Denver; we simply must continue to work together."

"Okay," nodded Harry, lighting a cigarette. "We've got to work fast, too."

"You mean you've some idea as to who Grey Moose is?"

"By this time tomorrow night, I hope to have a pretty good idea."

"You know where he'll be, then?" inquired Sir Richard, leaning forward eagerly in his chair and bending his paper-knife with nervous fingers.

"He'll be in the club room at the Kingfisher soon after ten. And I reckon we ought to look in on that meeting."

"We'll certainly do that," promised Sir Richard grimly. "How did you know about this?"

"I overheard it through the panel last night. They're fixing up another big job. It's so important that Big Chief will be there in person."

"You're absolutely certain about this – the time and place, I mean?"

"Miss Stone heard it as well. You can check with her at her office, if you like."

"No, no," said Sir Richard quickly. "That won't be necessary." He picked up the telephone and asked to be put through to one of the Flying Squad Inspectors … "Maxwell? … I shall want a couple of cars and – let me see – half a dozen men for eight sharp tomorrow night. We may pick up one or two extras locally … Yes, it's near Sevenoaks … Come round to my office when you've a minute and I'll give you the details." He slammed down the receiver and turned to Harry. "We've got to handle this carefully," he meditated. "This time he mustn't slip through our fingers …"

"You've got to keep your men out of sight," said Harry. "They'll have to pick up anyone who leaves … and you must have a couple at least watching White Towers. At ten o'clock they must force an entrance and come right down the underground tunnel to the Kingfisher."

"H'm, that seems pretty fool-proof. In the meantime, we close in on the pub and prevent anyone from leaving."

"You'll have to draw a pretty tight net," nodded Harry. "There may be still more ways out of that pub than we know of. Look at the way Sam Crawford vanished that day when one of your men caught sight of him in there. The main thing is to take them completely by surprise before they have time to organise any escape."

"They may have some escape plan already organised for just such an emergency," said McKendrick.

"In that case, we have to beat 'em to it! And if they get wind of this raid beforehand …" He hesitated.

"Eh? What's that?" said the Assistant Commissioner.

"If they get the low-down on our plans this time, Chief – well, I'll be the only man outside the Yard who's in on the secret."

"M'm …" murmured McKendrick. "I see what you mean."

CHAPTER NINETEEN

As he had not seen Diana all day, Harry telephoned her in the evening to make sure she had received no more unwelcome attentions from Grey Moose. But he said nothing about the raid on the Kingfisher, even when she tried to inquire about his future plans. She seemed quite cheerful, which she told him was largely due to an interesting day at the office and a particularly appetising supper devised by Mrs Bentley.

"By the way," she said, "I quite forgot to tell you that I had a letter this morning from your friend Mr Dancey."

"Dancey! I didn't know you'd met him."

"He wrote to me in my official capacity," she said. "He told me he was one of my regular readers and wondered if I could give him a little information."

"About what?"

"He's very anxious to trace a book published about fifty years ago."

"What sort of book?"

"It's called *Hideholes and Hidden Passages*, and he wanted me to print a request to readers to let him know of the whereabouts of a copy. Of course, I had to reply that it was against the policy of the feature. But it made me wonder if he's discovered that tunnel from the inn."

"I wouldn't worry too much about that if I were you," said Harry. "I've arranged for that passage to be watched pretty carefully."

"In what way?" she asked quickly.

"Never mind that, honey," he replied evasively. "If old Dancey is mixed up with that crowd I guess we'll find out pretty soon."

"Harry, you're holding out on me," she said reproachfully.

"Only for your own good," he assured her. "This is a full-sized man's job. Somebody's liable to get hurt."

"Oh dear! Harry, you will be careful, won't you?" There was no mistaking the note of anxiety in her tone.

"I said *somebody's* liable to get hurt," he repeated with a grin. "I guess I'll be behind the door if there's any rough stuff." He paused for a moment, then went on in a much more serious tone, "Diana, there's something else I want to tell you. I had a chat with Sir Richard about you today. I thought he should be told about that business with the record someone sent you."

"Well?"

"We agreed that someone should keep an eye on you."

"What does that mean, exactly?"

"He's going to put a plain-clothes man on to tailing you. Now, there's no need to get alarmed; it's just a precautionary measure. In fact, I was against telling you myself, but he thought you might get scared if you saw a strange man hanging around."

"There's something in that," she conceded. "What am I expected to do about all this?"

"You just relax and pay no attention whatever. In fact, I doubt if you'll notice this guy unless you particularly look out for him."

Again there was a pause. Then she said, "Well, thanks for telling me. I'll try not to panic."

"That's the girl!" laughed Harry. "And I'll call you on Sunday morning, if that's okay?"

"Anything you say," she murmured, burlesquing his intonation.

"Maybe I'll have some news then. And by the way, if you get any more parcels, don't open 'em!"

"I'll remember," she promised.

158

After he had replaced the receiver Harry lay back in his armchair and speculated for some minutes as to whether he had done the right thing in telling Diana that she was to be kept under observation. He told himself that he hadn't really had much experience of her type of woman; she was something special and you never knew quite how well she was going to take things. For instance, she'd gone through that underground tunnel almost without turning a hair, just as though it had been merely another newspaper assignment. He had come across one or two "sob sisters", as they called them during his brief newspaper days, but none of them had remotely resembled Diana Stone.

***

When the Assistant Commissioner and Inspector Rymer called for him the following evening, Harry insisted on their having a double whisky while they ran through a brief outline of the plan for the raid on the Kingfisher. Rymer produced a rough plan of the inn and its surroundings and they discussed the positioning of their men.

"By the way," said Harry, "I take it they'll be armed?"

"They are," replied Sir Richard promptly. "These men we're dealing with are dangerous, and we must leave nothing to chance. Don't you agree, Denver?"

"Sure, sure," murmured Harry, fingering his own automatic in his coat pocket, and hoping that the English police were not quite so ready to draw and not quite so erratic in their marksmanship as some Chicago cops of his acquaintance.

He turned to Rymer, who was due at White Towers, and gave him precise instructions as to the whereabouts of the statue and how it worked. He was to take four men with him down the tunnel, leaving two behind to deal with any sudden emergency that might arise. Harry could not help admiring the

159

brisk, unemotional manner in which Rymer disposed of all the details and settled any minor problems.

"You have your search warrant, Rymer?" queried McKendrick.

Rymer patted his breast pocket reassuringly. "I've got the warrants for both places," he replied.

"Good!" nodded McKendrick. "Well, take care in that passage – better move in single file, with a distance of two or three yards between you. And don't take any unnecessary chances. We've got enough men surrounding the inn to deal with a gang twice their size."

"We don't really know their strength, Sir Richard," Harry reminded him.

"We've no reason to expect more than half a dozen at the outside," replied Sir Richard. "But it isn't very important if one or two of the lesser lights escape, so long as we get Grey Moose."

"I quite understand, sir," nodded Rymer, preparing to take his leave.

"He seems a very efficient type," commented Harry when the Chief-Inspector had gone.

"A bit reserved," said Sir Richard, "but a wonderful organiser. He's only been at the Yard just over a year, but I don't mind admitting I should miss him." He drained his glass and refused another drink. "How much time have we got before we move off?" he inquired.

Harry glanced at his wristwatch. "Another ten minutes yet, Sir Richard. You said you'd have about nine or ten men surrounding the Kingfisher?"

"Yes, they should be there any minute now."

"What about the cars?"

"One will stop a little way down the road, the other will be near at hand."

Harry was just lighting a cigarette when the telephone rang. He heard Miles answering it in the hall outside.

Presently the butler came in and announced in dignified tones, "There's a Scottish lady for you on the telephone, sir – a Mrs Bentley. She says it's extremely urgent."

"Mrs Bentley?" repeated Harry, with some misgiving. "Put it through, will you, Miles?" He picked up the receiver from the instrument on the bureau.

"Is that you, Mr Denver?" came the familiar voice of Diana's housekeeper.

"Sure it's me, Mrs Bentley. Is anything wrong?"

"Yes, sir … it's about Miss Stone."

"Miss Stone?"

Sir Richard, who had been standing with his back to the fire, looked up swiftly as Harry repeated the name.

"Yes, sir," Mrs Bentley went on. "She isn't with you, by any chance, is she?"

"No, Mrs Bentley. I haven't seen her today. What time did she go out?"

"She had a phone call soon after ten this morning, while I was in the kitchen seeing about lunch. She seemed a wee bit flustered when she came in, and she said they wanted her round at the office right away but she'd be back in time for lunch. Since then I hav'na' heard a word from her."

"I wish you'd phoned before," reproved Harry.

"Och, I thought nothing of it at the time. She often misses a meal and sometimes forgets to phone and say she won't be in. I had to go out myself this afternoon to see my sister at Muswell Hill, but when I got back and saw there was no sign of Miss Diana I got worried and phoned the newspaper office. They said she'd been there this morning and left before lunch. That's all they knew – there was no message or anything."

"I see," said Harry, plainly taken aback.

161

"I'm sorry to trouble you, sir," continued the worried voice, "but Miss Diana did say I was to phone you if I thought anything was wrong any time."

"That's okay, Mrs Bentley. You did quite right. Leave this to me, and I'll call you back." He slammed down the receiver and said quickly, "Diana Stone's disappeared! What about the man who was tailing her?"

Sir Richard glanced at his watch. They still had over five minutes left before they were due to start for the Kingfisher. He rose, picked up the telephone, and asked to be connected to New Scotland Yard. When he had been put through to the office he required he said curtly, "Is there any report from Jackson?"

There was a pause, then a brief reply from the other end.

"H'mmm!" said McKendrick. "Well, tell Jackson right away that she isn't inside that building! He'd better get busy!" Sir Richard put down the receiver and turned to Harry. "Jackson followed her to the office all right, but he hasn't seen her since she went in. Come on, Denver, we'd better get moving or we'll be late."

CHAPTER TWENTY

They collected their coats in the hall and went out through the front door, where there was a Flying Squad car waiting for them. Sir Richard issued a curt direction to the driver, and they set off in the direction of the inn, keeping well within the 30 m.p.h. limit, for they were anxious not to attract undue attention.

Inside the car neither man spoke for a minute or so; they were obviously busy weighing up this new complication which had arisen.

At last Sir Richard broke the silence. "Do you think they've got her, Denver?"

Harry gazed moodily out of the window. "I guess there's something mighty peculiar going on, Sir Richard," he said at last.

"If they have kidnapped her they might have brought her down here."

"Not too easy in broad daylight," Harry reminded him.

"These devils seem to get away with anything," growled Sir Richard gloomily.

"Maybe we should concentrate on the job in hand," said Harry with a certain reluctance. "It may lead us to Diana in the end."

"Yes, yes, of course," nodded McKendrick, though he did not sound particularly confident.

At that moment the car drove round the side of the inn and backed into position in the car park so that it could make an instant getaway. Almost at once a figure loomed up from behind a nearby hawthorn hedge.

"Anything to report, Chambers?" asked McKendrick.

"No, sir. It seems very quiet. Not a soul about, in fact. We haven't seen anybody go in the pub since we got here."

"It's not a very popular pub," explained Harry. "Shall we go in now, Sir Richard?"

"All right," nodded the Assistant Commissioner. "Stand by, Chambers. Bring the men as close in as possible."

"They're moving in now, sir."

The moon had drifted sullenly beyond a bank of heavy cloud and there was a slight breeze stirring the trees as Sir Richard McKendrick and Harry Denver walked almost leisurely towards the front door of the inn. It was open and Harry led the way into the bar.

It was quite empty.

"What's the door on the opposite side of the passage?" Sir Richard whispered.

"It's the other bar. We'd better just look inside."

That too was deserted; so was the back sitting room.

"Looks like a wild goose-chase," grunted Sir Richard.

"There's something sinister about it," agreed Harry. *Somebody* should be on the premises."

"What's that door?" Sir Richard pointed.

"It leads out to the back – a little courtyard and strip of garden. Nothing much there except pigeon-cotes."

"It looks to me as if we were expected."

They went back to the larger bar and Harry indicated the door of the club room.

"Is that the room?" asked Sir Richard quietly.

Harry nodded.

McKendrick walked up to it and tapped lightly. "Anybody in there?" he called.

They stood in silence for ten seconds, waiting for an answer. Then Sir Richard nodded to Harry to stand clear, and he turned the knob of the door.

To their surprise, it opened quite readily. In the light reflected from the bar they could see nothing but a table and a few chairs. Harry found the switch and in a moment the club room was a blaze of light. But it was still as silent as the rest of the house.

"There's something damned mysterious about this," mused Sir Richard, walking slowly round the room, very much on the alert and in a much nervier state than he would have been had he encountered some signs of life. "Whereabouts is this panel leading to the secret passage?" he asked, and Harry indicated the cupboard against the far wall. Sir Richard went over to it and was just about to open the door when there was a gentle rumbling sound as the panel slid back.

"That'll be Rymer," said Harry.

Sir Richard opened the cupboard door wide and called out in a low, distinct tone, "Is that you, Rymer?"

"Yes, sir," came the reply, somewhat muffled by the robes in the cupboard.

"He hasn't wasted much time," commented Harry.

But Sir Richard was taking no chances, and he stood aside and waited until Rymer stepped into the room.

"How does that panel work?" inquired Harry curiously.

"Oh, it's quite simple, really," replied Rymer. "There's a little knob on the framework that releases a spring when you press it down."

Rymer's men emerged from the panel cautiously, one by one, as if they expected a hostile reception.

"There doesn't seem to be anyone here, Rymer," the Assistant Commissioner told him. "What about White Towers? Any trouble there?"

"No, sir. The place was deserted. But I'm afraid I found this on the table in the hall."

He handed his chief a plain gilt-edged card on which was typed:

ENTER SCOTLAND YARD – EXIT DIANA STONE.

Sir Richard passed it over to Harry, who read it without comment and gave it back.

"We'd better search the place thoroughly while we're about it," decided McKendrick. "Take your men upstairs, Rymer, and report at once if you find anything."

"Very good, sir." The Inspector was about to move off when he suddenly stood quite still. "I think I can hear somebody at the back, sir," he whispered.

Harry, who had also heard the footsteps, had already moved over to the door and was back in the bar just in time to see Inspector Bowen appear in the doorway.

"Good Lord, Sir Richard!" exclaimed Bowen, seeing his chief come up behind Harry. "What's going on here?"

"Evening, Bowen," said Sir Richard. "What brings you down here?"

"I came to see Denver. His man said he was up at the Kingfisher and –" He broke off as he saw more detectives emerging from the doorway. "What is all this? A raid of some sort?"

"Never mind now, Bowen. Did you want to see Denver urgently?"

"Yes, sir. I'm glad you're here … it's bad news."

Sir Richard turned to Rymer. "All right, take the men upstairs and let me know when you're through."

After they had gone Sir Richard closed both the doors. "Is this news something to do with me, too?" he asked.

"It certainly is, Sir Richard. I came down to see Denver because it concerns his friend Eric Trevelyan. He telephoned this evening just after you left to say that his shop had been burgled. The shop was closed this afternoon and … and –"

"Not the Brailsham Diamond?" queried Sir Richard quickly.

"No, sir. That went back to the safe deposit as soon as we knew the decoy plan had failed. But they got over twenty thousand pounds' worth of other stuff."

"Twenty thousand …" The Assistant Commissioner whistled softly under his breath.

Harry leaned his elbows on the bar and blew out a stream of cigarette smoke. "That was certainly a masterstroke, Sir Richard!" he declared. "Trevelyan's was just about the last place in London we'd expect them to choose. What time did it happen?"

"About six o'clock. They used gelignite to blow the safe, but there was hardly a soul about to hear the explosion. All the shops were closed, and they made a getaway without any trouble at all. Young Trevelyan actually saw them drive away without realising quite what had happened. He calls round about six every Saturday just to make sure everything's safely locked up for the weekend."

"What about the burglar alarms?" inquired Sir Richard.

"They're electric, and the gang took care of them simply by cutting off the current at the main. Taken all round, it was a very neat job."

"Yes," nodded Harry, stubbing out his cigarette on a large china ashtray, "they must have got wind of this raid, switched their meeting to last night, and planned that little coup there and then. Grey Moose can certainly pull off a neat little job of organisation in an emergency, I'll say that for him!"

"But how the devil could news of this raid have leaked out?" McKendrick protested. "Only the people immediately concerned were notified – I didn't even tell Bowen …"

"That's so," confirmed Bowen. "Otherwise I wouldn't have come barging in like this."

"It beats me," muttered McKendrick, rubbing his chin.

They eyed each other a trifle dubiously, as if they all dreaded that one would produce a *coup d'etat* at any moment.

167

They could hear heavy footsteps moving about overheard, but downstairs there was still no sign of life.

"I suppose I'd better tell Chambers the whole affair's a washout," said Sir Richard gloomily.

"Wait a minute!" interrupted Harry. "I think I can hear someone coming downstairs."

It was Rymer returning to report.

"There was the landlord's wife in her room, sir. She was fast asleep. She hasn't seen her husband all evening, and went to bed soon after closing time."

"I see," said Sir Richard. "Who else was up there?"

"An old gentleman was sitting up in bed, reading. When I told him you were here he insisted on seeing you. He's coming down now."

He turned to indicate the gentleman in question, clad in a most unsuitable dressing-gown of deep purple. Mr Benjamin Dancey came in smiling and holding out his hand. "Sir Richard – Mr Denver," he beamed, "how very nice to see you again."

CHAPTER TWENTY-ONE

Sir Richard looked more bewildered than ever. "Mr Dancey!" he exclaimed. "What the devil are you doing here?"

The little man smiled again, as imperturbable as ever. "You remember, Sir Richard. I told you last Sunday that I'm staying here for the time being, to investigate a Roman villa over at Chevening. I can assure you that the excavation has reached a most interesting stage. There's a fine mosaic –"

"Mr Dancey," interrupted the Assistant Commissioner in an irritable tone, "I am not in the least interested in Roman villas at the moment!"

Harry shot a warning glance at Sir Richard. "Perhaps I could have a word with Mr Dancey, sir," he said quietly, and turned to the grotesque little figure in the dressing-gown. "Mr Dancey, I've a pretty good idea of the real reason why you're staying here," he said softly. "What's more, I know who you are – and what you are."

"Indeed?" replied Mr Dancey with a certain dignity. "I'm afraid I don't quite follow you, Mr Denver."

"I guess we won't go into that now," replied Harry inscrutably. "All I want is the answer to the question – where is Diana Stone?"

"Diana Stone?" repeated the little man in some surprise. "The name is vaguely familiar. You mean the lady who writes in the *Daily Messenger*?"

"That's right," nodded Harry. "Her real name is Falconer, and she's the sister of the Superintendent who was murdered."

Mr Dancey was quite plainly taken aback. "F-Falconer!" he stammered. "Did Falconer really have a sister?"

"He certainly did," replied Harry briefly. "And what's more, she has disappeared."

There came an exclamation of surprise from Bowen, who was standing just behind Harry.

"When did this happen?" queried Rymer, in a tone which seemed to imply a measure of doubt.

"Her housekeeper telephoned me half an hour ago," Harry informed him.

"Mr Dancey," interposed Sir Richard. "Have you seen anyone come here tonight?"

"I'm afraid not, Sir Richard. I've been reading in my room for the greater part of the evening. In fact, I haven't been out of the house since teatime."

McKendrick was obviously becoming more and more irritated by the turn events had taken. He had wasted his time and that of a dozen men. It had been a wild goose chase, and he was feeling tired and frustrated. And on top of it all there was this news that the gang had pulled off another job right under their noses. This would mean more trouble; more awkward questions from politicians, sarcastic memoranda and talk of calling in "new blood". Maybe they were right; perhaps he was too old and ought to hand the job over to a more active mind ...

"You'd better take your party back to White Towers, Rymer," he said wearily, "and pick up your car there and go straight back to Town."

"Yes, sir," nodded Rymer, marshalling his men and returning to the club room.

"And if there's anyone returned when you get back to White Towers, question them closely about their movements this evening and make a full report."

"I quite understand, sir."

In a minute, the little party had disappeared.

Realising that Harry was anxious to see Mr Dancey alone, Sir Richard turned to Bowen and said, "Come along, Bowen, we'll have a word with Chambers. I'll be waiting in the car, Denver."

"Thank you, Sir Richard," said Harry gratefully. When the door had closed behind them Harry motioned Mr Dancey to a chair, then sat down himself.

Mr Dancey watched the two Scotland Yard men rather quizzically as they went out, then turned to Harry and asked, "Who was that with Sir Richard?"

"Inspector Bowen. You've probably seen him around here. He was watching the place for a couple of days after the murder."

"Ah, yes, I thought his face was familiar." Mr Dancey leaned back in his chair and eyed Harry thoughtfully. "I'm rather intrigued by that remark you made some time ago, Mr Denver. In fact, I might say I am *most* intrigued. Perhaps you can tell me a little more about myself?" There was a whimsical note in his voice.

"I know for one thing," said Harry, looking at him steadily, "that you have been known to do a deal in diamonds every now and then."

"How did you find that out?"

"Never mind that, Mr Dancey. I've got a lot of contacts in unexpected places."

Mr Dancey folded his hands across his stomach and said pleasantly, "It's quite true that I have a small stock of diamonds and I sell one from time to time."

"It's also true that you were never a schoolmaster; that for the past ten years, since you came from South Africa, you've made a living from buying and selling."

"Always within the law, Mr Denver – always within the law."

"I'm not disputing that," said Harry. "But why go to all this trouble to pose as an ex-schoolmaster dabbling in Roman remains?"

The little man looked round the room, then said in a low voice that could not possibly have been heard more than three feet away, "For precisely the same reason that Miss Diana Stone adopted the alias. We're up against a very unscrupulous man, Mr Denver, and he had a knack of penetrating into strange places. I have suffered from his diabolical methods in the past, and I have no intention of being caught again if I can help it."

Harry offered him a cigarette and lit one himself. "You knew Carl Kranston in South Africa?" he inquired casually.

Benjamin Dancey nodded his head slowly several times. There was a faraway look in his eyes. "I think I was one of Mr Kranston's earliest victims," he murmured, and there was a note of sadness in his voice. "He robbed me of a small fortune; it's many years ago now. I'd staked everything I had to go prospecting for diamonds, and after two years' bad luck I struck a nice little pocket. But Mr Kranston relieved me of most of them and left me for dead with a knife wound in the back. I'm very lucky indeed to be here to tell the tale."

"What happened to the diamonds?"

"He sold them and lost the money gambling."

"Do you think he'd know you again?"

The small man shook his head. "I very much doubt it. My hair had turned white … and my beard is new to him … and I've lost some weight. In any case, he only saw me for a couple of minutes when he rifled my tent – he'd never remember."

"And would you know him?"

"I'm afraid not," was the wistful reply. "You see, Mr Denver, he attacked me in the dark …"

"Then how do you know it was Carl Kranston?"

"That's rather a long story, I'm afraid. Let's say I made it my business to find out, just as I've made it my mission to help put an end to the career of this unscrupulous murderer. But he mustn't get a hint of my identity, Mr Denver. That's most important. And I trust no one; not even the police."

"Not even me?" queried Harry.

"Not altogether. I've had to tell you this because you've discovered a certain amount, and also because I think I may be able to help you to find Diana Stone before it's too late."

That ominous phrase sounded a jarring note on Harry's ears. Even now, at this very minute, he realised it might be too late.

Mr Dancey said, "I have no wish to be associated with the police, Mr Denver, in this affair, and I realise that it's more than possible that Sir Richard is planning to detain me on suspicion of being implicated in these gang robberies. If you can persuade him to hold his hand, then I think we stand an excellent chance of discovering the lady."

Harry surveyed him thoughtfully, from the tiny Arnold Bennett coif to the tips of his brown, pointed shoes. It was taking a chance; he suspected that Mr Dancey had several other matters he wished to conceal from the police. But things were desperate now. "Okay, Mr Dancey," he said deliberately. "I guess that little thing can be arranged."

With a little sigh of satisfaction Mr Dancey held out his hand.

"Well, that's all fine and dandy," said Harry, "but where do we go from here?"

"We go," declared Mr Dancey precisely, "to a place called Mincing Lane."

"Where on earth –"

"It's in the heart of the City of London," Mr Dancey informed him. "At least, it was …"

"Here, what goes on?" protested Harry.

"There was a meeting held in the club room here last night," continued Mr Dancey. "I'd taken the precaution of boring a hole, just a tiny hole, you understand – in the floor, and as soon as I realised what was afoot I did my best to overhear the conversation. Unfortunately, the hole was not in

173

a very favourable position and I could only catch an odd phrase or two. It wasn't until the end of the meeting that they moved in my direction and I overheard them refer to a hideout in some cellars opposite Plantation House in Mincing Lane. It seems that the entrance to the cellar is through an old courtyard and … Why, what's the matter?"

Harry Denver was on his feet and impatiently urging Mr Dancey to follow his example. "Get dressed as quickly as you can, Mr Dancey!"

The man seemed a trifle surprised. "You mean you'll take me with you?" he asked.

"Sure thing."

"You think there might be a – er – rough house?" queried Mr Dancey a little wistfully.

"Don't you worry about that. I'll take care of everything," Harry assured him.

"But I think I should come prepared …"

"I leave that to you," Harry shrugged.

Mr Dancey brightened perceptibly. "That's splendid! I purchased an ancient knuckle-duster only last week. Quite a formidable weapon, Mr Denver."

CHAPTER TWENTY-TWO

In a telephone box in Great Tower Street Sally Harrison stood talking in low, husky tones. From time to time she looked round to see if there was anyone outside who might possibly overhear, but there were very few people about in the City on a Saturday evening.

"Is that you, Carl? … Yes, it's me … No, no trouble as far as we know. It all went off like clockwork. Not so much stuff as we thought … About twenty thousand … Yes … The stuff will go at dawn tomorrow … Who? … Oh, yes, we've got her safe enough in the cellars. All right, Carl, leave it to me. Bye."

A cool evening breeze was blowing up tiny whirls of dust as she came out of the telephone box and approached the vast emptiness that was once the busy thoroughfare of Mincing Lane. In the past tea and coffee brokers had surged over the pavements selling the contents of their bulging warehouses and cellars. Nowadays Mincing Lane might almost have been a country thoroughfare, enclosed by fences one usually saw surrounding rural pastures. It was quite deserted now, and Sally walked on until she was almost level with Plantation House, scene of many a hectic auction. She looked round quickly and slipped behind a high board fence, to descend a flight of steps leading to the cellar.

Sally continued through the cellar, along a passage, and then turned sharply to the left, where two doors were immediately facing her. She chose the lefthand one, and went into a half-furnished room, where she switched on the light and flung herself on to the worn settee.

From time to time she glanced at the door as though she were expecting someone. She picked up a late edition of the evening paper and regarded it listlessly, re-reading the brief report of the jewel robbery in the stop press. She lighted a cigarette and stubbed it out before it was half smoked. Then she went to a small cupboard, took out a bottle of gin, and poured herself a generous measure.

She had not agreed with the chief's decision that they should move into this hide-out, but he had seemed very emphatic about it, and he did not always tell her the full details behind his moves. But she had to admit that it was an unusual retreat which was very unlikely to attract attention, for few people were seen nowadays in this part of the City, particularly after dark.

Sally was about to pour herself another drink when there was the sound of footsteps outside and the door opened. Dr Grant came in and carefully closed the door behind him.

"Where the hell have you been?" she snapped. "I told the chief the stuff was waiting to be sent off ages ago."

Grant pushed his hat back from his forehead with a weary gesture and began to unbutton his coat.

"We had a hell of a job with my car – had to change the back tyre," he replied, going to the cupboard and pouring himself a stiff whisky.

"Where's Joe and the others?" she inquired.

"Lew went to stow my car away. Joe and Bates are in the other car."

"You got the stuff through all right?"

He nodded. "Yes, that's all in order. By the way, what's happened about that girl?"

"Diana Stone? She's here."

"Here?" he echoed incredulously. "That's taking a hell of a risk, isn't it?"

"It was the chief's orders," she replied shortly. "That's all I know."

"Did she give any trouble?"

"She certainly did," replied Sally grimly. "Fought like blazes before I could get that cloth over her face. I think I kept it there a bit too long; she was a devil of a time before she came round."

Grant poured himself another liberal helping of whisky. He sat on the not very comfortable straight-backed chair opposite Sally and sipped his drink in silence.

"I want to have a talk with you, Doc, before the rest of the boys get here," Sally said.

"That suits me," he agreed. "In fact, I sent them to park the car so that I could have a word with you."

"Well?" she said, with a note of challenge of her voice.

Grant leaned back in his chair and thoughtfully regarded his glass. "No doubt you can guess what I want to say."

"I haven't the least idea," she replied indifferently.

"Then I'll tell you," he replied, though he seemed to find it a trifle difficult. "You know as well as I do, of course, that six months ago I was an unpaid doctor on a fourth-rate tramp steamer from Argentina. Then one night in Scotland Road, Liverpool, I happened to come across the chief, whom I'd met some years previously in Marseilles. He told me he had the very job for me and I was only too glad to give it a trial. Of course, I suspected right from the start that it wouldn't be strictly legal, but I'd no idea then that it would be such a money-maker."

"What's all this in aid of?" she demanded restlessly.

"I'm trying to tell you that whereas six months ago I should hardly have cared if my tramp steamer had gone to the bottom, I've rather changed my point of view since then. For the first time in some years I'm actually looking to the future!"

"What am I supposed to do about that?"

"Nothing at all, my dear Sally, as long as you don't do anything to upset my plans." He hesitated for a moment, then added significantly, "The same applies to your friend Grey Moose."

The trend of his remarks suddenly became obvious to her. "Why do you think Grey Moose would want to interfere?" she asked.

Grant shrugged. "We know what's happened to three members of our little set-up," he murmured. "All very neat, very timely, and highly efficient ... but very unfortunate for the individuals concerned."

Sally took a sip at her glass. "Why should you worry?" she said. "It's paid a good dividend, hasn't it?"

"Yes," he smiled grimly. "It pays a good dividend to those who remain alive to draw it. And I have made certain that I shall be one of them."

Sally looked puzzled. "What are you getting at?"

"I'm merely trying to tell you that I have taken certain precautions against anything happening to me."

"Nothing will happen to you if you do as you're told," she replied curtly.

"Nothing will happen to me in any case," he asserted deliberately. "If by any chance I should be the victim of an unfortunate accident I've made all arrangements with a very reliable firm of family solicitors to deliver a letter direct to the Home Secretary. You won't need to be told that there's quite a lot of vital information in that letter."

"You damned fool!" she exclaimed desperately. "If you dare to –"

"It's not a question of my daring to do anything, my dear adopted niece. The initiative lies solely with your gentleman friend. That letter will neither be opened nor posted unless I die in circumstances necessitating an Inquest."

Her lips narrowed into a cruel line, and there was a note of contempt in her tone as she said, "Carl has no intention of double-crossing you. You're much too valuable. He never gets rid of your sort ... but the others ..."

"What about the others?"

She hesitated a moment, then said slowly, "The chief has decided they've got to go."

"Why?"

"That was our last big job tonight, and the chief has been tipped off that there are warrants out for all of us except himself. Somebody overheard our meeting in the club room on Thursday. So you see, if any of the others are picked up they're almost certain to talk, and we can't take any chances on that."

Grant said, "Perhaps you're right. But, frankly, I don't like it, Sally."

"It's the chief's orders," she reminded him. "As soon as we can get away he wants us to fly to Cannes. He'll join us there some time during next week. There'll be another ten thousand each for us over there."

Grant drank the rest of his whisky and considered the proposition. "What about this girl, Diana Stone?" he said presently.

"The chief will take care of her."

"Why did he bring her here? I'm damned if I can see any point in it."

Sally shrugged her elegant shoulders and said, "Because she happens to be the sister of Superintendent Falconer."

"Phew!" This was plainly news to Grant. "You mean the man who was killed at the Kingfisher?"

"That's the man. He was right on our tail; he knew Carl in South Africa, and he was dangerous. The girl knows too much. So does Mr Harry Denver."

"Yes, I shall have to deal with Mr Denver," the doctor said grimly.

"Don't worry, he can't do a thing while we've got the girl," she assured him.

"Have you heard from the chief?"

179

"Yes, I rang him up to tell him we were here and that the Bond Street job was all okay."

"We haven't got the stuff out yet," he reminded her. "There may still be plain-clothes men hanging around the Kingfisher."

"We'll deal with that all right," she replied confidently.

For a few minutes neither spoke. He gazed unseeingly through half-closed eyes as he turned over the plans in his mind, visualising himself living a pleasantly retired life at Cannes. Then he spoke suddenly. "All right – what's the scheme?"

"Come this way."

She led him out of the room and through the adjacent door which admitted them to a flight of steps leading to another cellar. She produced a small electric torch, and in a little alcove leading off the passage the beam revealed a large wooden flap built into the floor. They drew back the bolts and lifted it a few inches. Almost at once a rushing of waters was audible.

"It's a big culvert that runs into the Thames," she announced.

They let the flap fall and looked at each other in silence for several seconds.

Then the doctor nodded. "It seems pretty safe," he decided.

They retraced their steps and as they came to the foot of the cellar steps he asked her where the girl was.

"In the second room along there," she replied, nodding towards the passage. "She's safe enough."

"All right. I think I can handle this."

She placed her hand on his arm for a moment and said softly, "You won't regret it."

They continued up the stairs and into the room she had first entered.

"What are you going to do?" she asked quickly as he closed the door and crossed to the cupboard.

Opening it he took out the whisky bottle and three clean glasses and placed them on a small, cheap table which stood against the wall and served as a sideboard. He held the bottle up to the light and saw that it was three-quarters full. Then, from an inside pocket, he took out a dark green phial.

"What's that?" she inquired curiously.

"Just a little something to give an extra kick to the whisky," he replied with a sinister smile. "I've been saving it for an occasion like this. Incidentally, it's very difficult to trace at a post-mortem – not that that need worry us unduly."

Very deliberately he unscrewed the stopper and slowly emptied the colourless fluid into the whisky.

"And that's that!" he said, replacing the stopper and slowly tilting the whisky bottle.

"Are you sure they all drink whisky?" she asked.

"They won't get anything else," he assured her. "And I've never known them refuse it before." He took her glass and his own and filled them up with gin and orange from the bottles in the cupboard. "We must drink ourselves as if everything's quite normal," he instructed her. "Just watch me closely and appear as natural as possible."

"There won't be any – struggle or –" she began apprehensively, but he shook his head.

"Practically instantaneous," he said emphatically.

There came the sound of footsteps descending the stone steps outside, and presently they heard a firm double knock on the door.

"Come in!" called Sally, picking up her glass.

CHAPTER TWENTY-THREE

"Why, hello, Joe," said Sally with a smile. "We wondered what had happened to you. We thought you were coming with Bates."

Joe scowled and pushed the door shut with his foot. "This is a hell of a place!" he mumbled.

"Something upset you, Joe?" hazarded Grant shrewdly.

Joe wiped his hand over his mouth with an expressive gesture. "I'll say it has," he muttered. "I 'aven't 'ad a chance to tell either of you before, but when we made the getaway it was all dead easy till a rozzer tried to stop us down Brixton Road. They must 'ave put the alarm out by then, and he looked as if he meant business. Even then we'd have been all right if George 'and't lost his nerve and started shoutin'. Before you could say knife the rozzer was tryin' to jump onto the bonnet. There was nothin' else to do – I swerved and he fell right off in front of a lorry – My God, it was awful!"

"You damn fool!" exclaimed the doctor. "This'll mean more trouble. They'll put out a description of that car and –"

"What the hell could I do?" snapped Joe in a surly tone. "We were in a jam. I changed the number plates as soon as we'd got clear." He slumped down on the settee and said thickly, "I'm just about all in! What about a drink?"

Grant eyed him closely. "You've had a few already," he said.

"And what if I 'ave? I reckon I needed 'em."

"All right," said Grant. "There's some whisky. Help yourself."

Joe slouched over to the small table and poured himself three generous fingers of whisky. "George was in a terrible state – and still is, for that matter," he said as he recorked the bottle. "He popped into that pub along the way for a quick one to steady 'im a bit." With the glass halfway to his lips he said, "Have you heard from the chief?"

"Yes," replied Sally. "He'll be in touch with us later."

Joe nodded, then seemed about to say something more, but Grant intervened and lifted his glass.

"Cheerio, Joe! Here's to some more paying jobs like this!"

Joe took a prolonged gulp at his whisky and drew in a deep breath. "Yes," he said, "I don't mind tellin' you that was one of the neatest bits of work I –" His features seemed to contract and he pressed both hands over his heart. His breath came in great gasps and he flopped heavily on to the worn settee.

Grant and Sally stood looking at him without moving an inch. Neither made any attempt to help him.

For a moment or two Joe rocked from side to side, obviously in severe pain. Perspiration had broken out on his forehead and streamed down his face.

Grant nodded to Sally. "Open the door and give me a hand," he said quietly.

She did as he asked, and Grant took the inert body by the shoulders and started to drag it towards the door. Sally shone her torch down the cellar steps. The lifeless feet slithered and clattered down the stairs as Grant descended. Sally had the flap already open by the time he reached it.

He paused for a moment, breathing hard. "Help me to look through his pockets, just in case …"

They did so very quickly, but found nothing of any importance. Satisfied, Grant rolled the body towards the opening and gave it a final push. He closed the flap and dusted himself down.

"That's the last we'll see of him," he murmured, half to himself.

They returned to the sitting room, and Grant looked at Sally rather curiously. She did not seem in the least upset. As a doctor he was accustomed to death and other disturbing sights, but he was mildly surprised that this girl seemed as indifferent as he was himself to the spectacle of Joe's violent end.

In a matter-of-fact way Sally straightened the ruffled carpet, then picked up Joe's glass which had fallen to the floor. Grant took the glass, wiped it with his handkerchief, and put it back in the cupboard.

"The other two should be here any minute now," Grant said casually.

Sally picked up the whisky bottle, looked at it, and set it down again on the table. "What is that stuff?" she inquired again.

"I don't think you'd be much wiser if I gave you the chemical formula," he replied with the ghost of a smile. "Why do you ask?"

She shrugged. "On this game, one never knows when a quick way out might be useful …"

He was about to say something when she held up her hand for silence and they heard footsteps approaching.

"That'll be Lew and George," she said, picking up her glass.

When the two arrived Grant and Sally were sipping their drinks and apparently engaged in a casual conversation.

The landlord was obviously still very much on edge. "Hello, Doc!" he said nervously, looking round the room and nodding to Sally. He took off his worn trilby and twisted it in his stubby fingers.

"Oh, there you are, George," said the doctor. "Where's Joe?"

"Isn't he here yet?" asked Bates in some surprise. "I thought he came on ahead of us."

184

"That's right," nodded Lew Paskin, speaking for the first time.

"Oh, well, perhaps he stopped somewhere for a drink after he'd put the car away," suggested the doctor equably.

"Wasn't he supposed to be with you, George?" asked Sally.

"We 'ad a bit of trouble and did a quick change-over," exclaimed George Bates somewhat shiftily, placing a small attaché case on the table.

"What have you got there?" asked Grant.

"It's the stuff – all of it …"

"But I distinctly told you it was to be left at the Kingfisher."

"I'm trying to tell you," protested Bates hoarsely. "There was plain-clothes men all over the place when we got there. Luckily Lew spotted one of their cars, so we turned back right away and come straight 'ere. Nothin' else we could do. I 'ad to bring the stuff with me."

Grant looked questioningly at Sally, who gave him a barely perceptible nod and proceeded to open the little case.

The stuff was certainly there; a pair of diamond earrings worth three thousand pounds and a necklace of small but exquisitely matched pearls. Sally picked up a platinum ring, examined it for a moment, then returned it to the pile.

"I suppose it will be safe enough here," said Grant rather doubtfully. "Did Joe give you the list?"

"There's no list here," said Sally, searching inside the case.

"No, Joe 'ad it. Where on earth's 'e got to?" said the landlord.

"I expect he's a bit nervy after that spot of bother you had, George," Grant observed.

George Bates looked up quickly. "'Ere, who told you about that? 'Ow did you know there'd been some bother?"

185

Grant stalled for a moment, but the girl came to his rescue.

"The chief told me on the phone," she said. "He'd picked up a police radio message."

George Bates looked more scared than ever. "A police message!" he repeated in a hoarse undertone. "Did 'e say if they'd got the car number?"

"They gave a description, but no number."

"Ah," said the innkeeper, relaxing a little. "Well, I reckon we've earned a drink."

He made a move towards the whisky, but before he could reach it there was a piercing scream from somewhere in the cellars. It sounded particularly eerie as it echoed along the passage and faded into silence.

"What the 'ell's that?" exclaimed George Bates.

"It's all right," said Grant reassuringly. "Nothing to be alarmed about." He took a large handkerchief from his pocket and passed it to Sally. "Tie it tightly this time!" he ordered.

"Leave it to me," she said, and went out quickly.

"Who've you got out there?" asked Lew Paskin.

"It's a girl named Diana Stone."

"What's she doin' 'ere? This is no time to 'ave women screamin' the place down," George Bates declared. "Somebody outside might 'ave 'eard ..."

"There's nothing to worry about," Grant affirmed. "The chief had her brought here because she's dangerous – she knows too much."

"What's he goin' to do with 'er?"

Grant shrugged. "He just said hold her for the time being."

"I don't like it," said Paskin.

"It's really no business of ours," replied Grant pointedly. "What you two need is a nice stiff whisky. Go on, help yourselves."

186

"Well, I wouldn't say no to a snifter," admitted Bates.

Lew Paskin poured himself a drink and passed the bottle to Bates, who very nearly filled his glass.

As they were about to drink, Sally re-entered the room.

"We won't be hearing from that young lady again just yet awhile," she announced in a satisfied tone.

"Good," said Grant. "Will you join us in a drink, Sally?"

"I've still got some gin left," she smiled, holding up her glass. "Why, what's the matter, George?"

George Bates had suddenly uttered an expressive exclamation. "I've left those blasted number plates in the back of the car! If it was searched ..." He put down his glass and went towards the door. "I reckon I'd better get rid of 'em right away."

"Where are you going to put them?" she asked.

"Anywhere ... plenty of heaps of rubble round 'ere ... I'll stow 'em out of the way somewhere. Shan't be five minutes."

Sally looked across at Grant as George Bates departed, and gave a tiny shrug.

"I should hide that stuff away somewhere," advised Lew, indicating the attaché case. "Well, cheerio!" He lifted his glass and drank more than half its contents.

Lew Paskin was not such a sturdy man as Joe Wilcox and the poison seemed to do its deadly work even more rapidly.

Once again Sally and Grant followed the same procedure, though rather more quickly for Paskin was considerably lighter in weight.

As they replaced the trap door Sally asked, "What are we going to tell Bates?"

Grant brushed the dust from the knees of his trousers. "I'll tell him Lew's with the girl," he decided, and they retraced their way up the steps.

"Shall I fill up Lew's glass?" she asked when they were straightening the room.

He shook his head. "George Bates knows Lew would never leave an un-emptied glass behind him. Better empty out what's left."

She did as he suggested, returning the remains of Lew's drink to the whisky bottle.

"I must say I never thought you had it in you, Doc," she said quietly as they waited for Bates to return.

His lips set in a tight, expressionless smile for a moment, then he replied quickly, "If it comes to that, I'd no idea you could be quite so tough."

At that moment they heard Bates approaching and picked up their glasses.

"Did you get rid of them all right, George?" asked the doctor as Bates came in.

"Yes, I stowed 'em away under a heap of old scrap iron that looked as if it'd been there for years." He paused and looked round the room. "'Allo, what's 'appened to Lew?"

"Oh, he went downstairs to have a look at the girl. He wanted to see if she was the same one who called at White Towers this week," answered Grant easily.

"'E'll never learn to keep 'is nose out of things that don't concern 'im," declared George Bates.

The doctor leaned over and passed him a glass. "Oh, well, he'll be back in a minute. Here's your drink."

Bates took the glass and set it down on the table beside him.

"I can't 'elp feelin' a bit worried about that rozzer. He 'ad a good look at both of us. Did the radio message say 'e'd snuffed it?"

"The chief didn't say," answered Sally.

The innkeeper shuffled his feet uncomfortably and looked from one to the other, a thoughtful frown creasing his none too clean features. "What the devil is Lew doin'?" he demanded irritably. "I can't 'ear any sound of talking ..."

"For one thing, the lady is heavily gagged," smiled Sally, "and for another, they'd be too far away for you to hear anything less than a shout or scream."

"Well, I wish 'e'd 'urry up and come back," sniffed Bates, fumbling in his pocket and taking out a cigarette.

"You're pretty jumpy, George," said Grant soothingly. "Why don't you have a drink to steady your nerves?"

But George Bates made no effort to take the hint. "What about the doings for the Brighton job?" he grumbled. "That was to 'ave come through in time for the last meetin'."

"The chief will be along with it tonight," explained Sally. "He told me on the phone that your cut will be just on five thousand."

"Five thousand!" Bates whistled. "By God, I'll paint the ruddy town red! And after that I'll get out of that stinkin' pub and get me a nice little place at Brighton – near the racecourse – see a bit o' life there."

Grant smiled. "That's fine!" he said, raising his glass. "Here's luck to the new pub!" He took a sip at his drink, but George Bates did not join him. "What's the matter with you?" he asked peevishly. "Have you gone on the wagon?"

George Bates gave a mirthless little chuckle "Me on the wagon! That'd be a fine start to runnin' a new pub, that would!"

"Then drink up, George, and toast the new venture," smiled Sally, raising her glass.

But George Bates's whisky remained untouched. He and the doctor eyed each other.

"What's the matter?" Grant asked at last. "Why aren't you drinking?"

For a moment the innkeeper did not reply. Then he rose slowly to his feet and with a sudden movement produced a revolver from an inside pocket. "Because I'm no sucker!" he snarled.

Dr Grant took an involuntary step backwards, and Bates construed it as a move to escape. "You keep away from that door," he said threateningly, "or I'll blow your blasted brains out! Don't think I 'aven't got a good idea what's in that glass."

"Put down that gun, George, and don't be a damned fool," advised the doctor calmly. "There's nothing wrong with that drink."

"No?" said Bates sarcastically. "All right then, *you* drink it."

"I tell you it's harmless … Your nerves are just on edge …"

"Of course it's harmless," said Sally.

"All right," Bates challenged, swinging round on her, "then *you* drink it!"

"You know I never touch whisky."

George Bates laughed sardonically. "In that case, it's the doc who'll 'ave to oblige." With his left hand he slid the glass along the table in the doctor's direction. "But before you drink it, tell me what you've done with Lew and Joe," he ordered, waving his revolver.

"I told you we haven't seen Joe," Grant said, somewhat shakily.

"Come on now – I want the truth!"

"Now listen to me, George," Grant began, using a persuasive tone.

"I'm not listenin' to you – I'm tellin' you! I don't want any of this soft soap business. What's 'appened to those two? You can tell me the truth or drink this whisky!"

Grant backed a step, but to his surprise Sally came forward and picked up the glass.

"You know I loathe whisky," she said calmly, "but just to satisfy you, George, I'll drink half of it."

"Garn! You wouldn't dare!" retorted Bates with disbelief.

"We've told you it was nothing but whisky," she said. "All right, I'll prove it."

Slowly she raised the glass to her lips, but before it touched them she twisted her wrist and flung the contents full into Bates's face. For a moment he was blinded, and in that instant Grant snatched up the whisky bottle and brought it down on Bates's head.

"Thanks, Sally!" gasped Grant. "That was a near thing." He seemed momentarily exhausted by his sudden effort, but presently he stooped and examined the inert form.

"Listen!" said Sally suddenly. "Isn't that a car?"

They waited for the slamming of the car doors, but heard nothing.

"Better move him out of sight, just in case," decided Grant. "Could you give me a hand?"

Together they lifted George Bates and pushed him behind the settee. But they were not quite quick enough.

"You really shouldn't go to all that trouble," said a polite voice from the doorway, and they swung round to see Mr Dancey standing there.

For five seconds there was complete silence, then Grant said quietly, "Come in, Mr Dancey. Come in and close the door."

Mr Dancey did so without taking his eyes off them. "Let me see, you will be Dr Grant. I think we met on the night of – er – that deplorable affair at the Kingfisher."

"That is so, Mr Dancey."

"And this, no doubt, is your charming niece that I've heard so much about," continued Mr Dancey imperturbably.

"You seem to know quite a lot about it," Grant said, with just a barely audible edge to his voice. "But you haven't told us anything about yourself."

"It's very kind of you to inquire," smiled Mr Dancey amiably. "I'll be delighted to oblige. What exactly do you want to know about me?"

"Suppose you begin by telling us precisely who you are, and what you are doing here tonight?"

"But surely our old friend, Bates, told you who I am. I'm Benjamin Dancey, a retired schoolmaster, interested in antiques, and almost anything from a bygone age. As you know, I've been staying at the Kingfisher, exploring the local countryside, and I have come across the remains of a most interesting Roman villa at Chevening that –"

"Yes, yes," interposed Grant, now slightly suspicious that for some reason Dancey was playing for time, "but that doesn't explain why you are here."

"But I should have thought that would be obvious, my dear Doctor. This place is teeming with ancient relics. Why, just along the way is the most remarkably preserved Roman bastion that is quite unbelievable! I assure you that it is well worth a visit. In fact, I'm surprised you haven't seized the opportunity long before this to –"

"You don't look at ruins at this time of night," interrupted Sally coldly, her eyes narrowing.

"I assure you those old buildings look quite different by moonlight. There's a poem by Scott on the subject –"

"There is no moon tonight," Sally pointed out.

At that moment Mr Dancey noticed that Grant was covering him with the automatic which had fallen from George Bates's hand. "Really, Doctor Grant, is that necessary?" he said, mildly reproving.

The doctor made a threatening movement. "We are still waiting for you to answer our questions, Mr Dancey. What are you doing here?"

"Please be careful with that revolver; it's a most dangerous weapon," Dancey said a little apprehensively.

"I'm glad you appreciate that. Now, for the last time, will you answer my question?"

"Certainly, certainly. I came to look for a lady whom I understand is being detained here."

"What's her name?"

Mr Dancey hesitated, and the doctor repeated the question.

"I believe," said Mr Dancey, "that her professional name is Miss Diana Stone."

Grant sat back on the edge of the table. "I see," he nodded. "And may I ask how you knew that she was here?"

"Really, Doctor, that's rather a long story."

"Then you'd better tell it quickly. There's no time to lose."

Mr Dancey looked from one to the other with a remonstrating air. "I must ask you to believe that Miss Stone is really only an acquaintance – yes, indeed, the merest acquaintance," he began mildly. "I read something in a recent column of hers about ancient buildings, and I wrote her a little note – "

"This is leading nowhere," broke in Sally. "He's just stalling for time." She nodded to Grant, who motioned Mr Dancey back towards the door.

"Come along, then, Mr Dancey, he said suavely. "We'll take you to meet your friend Miss Stone."

Mr Dancey looked round nervously.

"Open the door!" commanded Grant.

Slowly Mr Dancey turned the knob and pulled the door towards him. As it opened, he stood behind it, leaving a clear view of the doorway and the sight of Harry Denver standing there holding an automatic.

"Drop that gun, Grant!"

With a metallic clank the doctor's revolver fell to the floor.

Sally glanced across at him with contempt. "How did you get in here?" she asked.

"With Mr Dancey," replied Harry curtly. "And that's the last question from you, my friend. I'm getting a bit tired of monkeying around with your crowd, and I guess this affair's going to be cleared up right now. Come on in, Diana, and give us a hand."

Diana came up behind him and entered the room. She looked pale and there was a cut on her cheek and ominous red marks on her wrists. Her hair was untidy, but there was a triumphant gleam in her eye and she moved with a quiet intensity.

"Pick up that revolver, will you, Diana?" asked Harry.

"I'm very much afraid there is a – er – body behind the settee," murmured the gentle voice of Mr Dancey. "I just caught sight of a man's foot as I came into the room."

"Move out the settee then, will you, Mr Dancey?"

"Oh dear," muttered the little man, as he did so. "It's Mr Bates. He seems to have a very nasty head wound; I doubt if he'll recover consciousness for some time. He should have instant attention, Mr Denver."

"He'll have to wait," decided Harry.

"What are we going to do with them?" asked Diana, indicating Grant and Sally.

"Take 'em downstairs and tie 'em up in the room where I found you," Harry answered. "You go on ahead and I'll bring up the rear. And don't hesitate to shoot if there's any nonsense." He turned to the two captives. "Miss Harrison – Dr Grant – you heard what I said."

"Just a minute," put in Mr Dancey. "Are you forgetting this?" He indicated the attaché case on the table.

Still keeping Grant and Sally covered, Harry examined the pile of jewellery. He whistled softly. "The Trevelyan job … Quite a nice little haul, eh, Doctor?"

Grant made an involuntary movement, but Harry's Colt waved him back.

"I think perhaps you'd better stay here, Mr Dancey, and keep an eye on this stuff," Harry said. "We'll be back in five minutes, then we'll prepare to receive a certain distinguished visitor." He looked across at Sally as he said this, but she avoided his eye.

"Certainly, I'll wait here," agreed Mr Dancey, settling himself as comfortably as possible and taking a much used briar pipe from one pocket and a folded newspaper from the other. He was settling back to read it as Harry and Diana shepherded their prisoners from the room and out into the passage.

Harry produced his torch and they soon found their way down to the room where Diana had been tied to a chair. There were still several lengths of rope lying around, and Harry tied up his captives very efficiently.

Diana was beginning to look rather tired and she was very glad when this unpleasant task had been completed. Harry gagged both Grant and the girl, using his own handkerchief and the one that he had untied from Diana's mouth when he had released her.

As they closed the door behind them Diana whispered, "What are we going to do now, Harry?"

"Wait for Grey Moose," he replied almost nonchalantly.

"What makes you so sure he'll come?"

"For one thing to see you; for another to pick up that stuff from Trevelyan's. By the way, did you happen to overhear them say anything about that job?"

She shook her head. "They didn't talk very much … though I did happen to catch one stray phrase that sounded queer."

"What was it?"

"Something about "Release at dawn" …"

195

"Release at dawn," he repeated thoughtfully. "That seems to ring a bell."

"What's it mean?"

"We'll sort it out, all in good time," he assured her as they quietly climbed the cellar steps and moved towards the room where they had left Mr Dancey. "As soon as we've dealt with our visitor I'll phone the Yard and –" He broke off and stood stock-still, gripping her wrist. "That's *my* car!" he exclaimed, as they heard the unmistakable roar of an engine, and with flying leaps he went bounding up the basement steps. But he was only just in time to see a rapidly disappearing tail light turn into Great Tower Street and vanish.

"Harry – who could it have been?" cried Diana. She had followed him up the steps and now stood by his side, shivering in the night air.

Harry remained lost in thought for a few moments. Then he said, "There's always a chance it might have been some car thief who saw it standing there with no-one about. I'll phone the Yard and get 'em to put out a description. Come on, honey, let's see if our Mr Dancey is ready."

They retraced their footsteps and returned to the sitting room.

Harry went in first, and almost at once he turned and stretched out his arm to restrain Diana from following him. He realised that the man they had been waiting for had already left.

There was no sign of the attaché case containing the spoils of the Trevelyan robbery, but slumped against the table, with a stiletto in his back, lay Benjamin Dancey.

CHAPTER TWENTY-FOUR

By a stroke of good fortune they discovered a City policeman on duty at the corner of Great Tower Street and sent him back to the cellar to take charge of Grant and Sally Hamilton.

Harry went into the same telephone box which Sally had used a couple of hours previously and was immediately connected to New Scotland Yard. Unfortunately Sir Richard McKendrick had left an hour earlier. Harry then put in a call to Sir Richard's home address in Hampstead, and after a short delay the Assistant Commissioner came to the telephone.

"Hello, Denver," said the familiar voice. "We've been wondering what's happened to you."

Harry gave him a very rapid résumé of the events of the evening.

"H'm, you've certainly been busy," commented the Assistant Commissioner grimly. "Is Miss Stone all right?"

"She's okay," said Harry, "and I guess we've pretty near broken up that gang."

"But we still haven't got Grey Moose."

"You said it! Maybe we will yet, though. I've still got a card or two up my sleeve."

"Well, for heaven's sake let's get busy," said McKendrick. "Is there anything you want me to do?"

"Yes, first of all have Grant and the girl taken in. I told the officer I saw not to budge till you sent someone along."

"Right, I'll attend to that," promised Sir Richard. "We ought to get some useful information out of them. They know the identity of Grey Moose, of course."

"They sure do. But whether you can make 'em talk is quite another matter. That Grant guy's a tough customer, and the girl wouldn't say a word if you tortured her with hot irons."

"What makes you say that?"

"I've been getting the dope on her. She's Carl's special girl friend – follows him round the world. I guess they've just been planning the big getaway – that's if their past routine is anything to go by."

"Humph! Well, is there anything else you want me to do?"

"Yes, I'd like you to arrange with your Sevenoaks people to let me have two or three men early tomorrow morning."

"I'll get Bowen to fix that up right away."

"There's no need to trouble Bowen or anyone at the Yard," Harry assured him. "You could get through to the Inspector at Sevenoaks and arrange it direct with him."

"Well, of course, if you say so," said Sir Richard, sounding slightly doubtful. "You're sure you wouldn't prefer a Squad car?"

"No, no, just a couple or three reliable men from the local station will be ample. I shall want them down at my place fairly early – not later than five."

"What's going on?" inquired Sir Richard curiously.

"I'm afraid I can't answer that one just yet. I'm simply acting on a hunch, you see."

"It all sounds very mysterious," said the Assistant Commissioner.

"Maybe," replied Harry. "Anyway, I guess it's about my last chance of getting my hands on the stuff from Trevelyan's and the man who organised the job. And I'd take it as a favour, Sir Richard, if you didn't mention this to a soul – except the Inspector at Sevenoaks, of course. Three men, at my place, at five sharp."

"Are you sure three will be enough?"

"Pretty sure," Harry replied. "George Bates won't be fit for much, and from what Diana tells me I guess Grant and the girl bumped off Wilcox and Paskin before we got there tonight. I've a feeling we're coming mighty close to the final curtain."

"All right, Denver, you shall have your men at five o'clock."

"Thanks, Sir Richard." Then Harry added as an afterthought, "By the way, I almost forgot to mention that Grey Moose stole my car. It's a red saloon – a three-and-a-half litre Columbia. I guess he's abandoned it by now, but I'd like to get it back as soon as possible."

"I'll see to it," Sir Richard promised. "And, Denver –"

"Yes, Sir Richard?"

"You'll be careful, won't you? This man is sure to be armed and desperate."

"I can still hit the ace of hearts at ten yards," chuckled Harry. "Good night, Sir Richard, I'll phone you first thing in the morning."

"Good night, Denver – and good luck!"

Harry came out of the telephone box, and Diana, who had been standing in the shadows, rejoined him. They looked around for a taxi, but the City on a Saturday night is as deserted as a country lane, and they set out to walk briskly in a westerly direction.

"Are you sure we oughtn't to go back to – that place, to make a statement to the police and see that everything is all right?" she asked.

"Sir Richard will look after all that. He'll send a Squad car to pick up Grant and Sally Harrison; there's already a warrant out for them. We'll make a full statement tomorrow."

"Then what do we do now?"

"You go to bed and get a good night's sleep and try to forget everything," he advised. "I'm going to do the same, because I must be up long before the crack of dawn tomorrow."

As the dome of St Paul's loomed towards them they caught sight of an empty bus going towards Ludgate Hill and managed to race it to the nearest stop. It happened to be a Number 11, which would take Diana almost to her door. They climbed the stairs and sat in the two seats at the back on the top deck, where they both lighted cigarettes. For some minutes they sat without speaking, drawing in and expelling long streams of tobacco smoke.

"Well, I guess this is one day of my life I wouldn't like to live over again," said Harry presently.

"Me, too," she nodded. "How ever did you manage to find me in that awful place, Harry?"

"It was old Dancey who put me on the track, or I wouldn't have had an idea," he told her.

"Poor old Dancey. It's dreadful to think it cost him his life."

"Yes," said Harry. "That's one more good reason why I've got to level scores with Grey Moose."

She sighed. "He's always a move ahead of us, Harry. It almost seems like thought-reading or some strange sort of trick."

"It won't always come off," he assured her. "Even tonight he had a pretty near squeak. Maybe next time …"

She shivered slightly at the prospect. Then she asked, "Why do you think he disappeared tonight, after he'd stabbed Mr Dancey? He must have known Grant and Miss Harrison were somewhere in the cellars."

Harry flicked the ash off his cigarette. "I think Grey Moose made a pretty shrewd guess at what had happened," he said. "The fact that Dancey was guarding that stuff would have given him a tip that there was something unpleasant going on. Besides, we don't know how much information he got out of Dancey before he killed him – he probably told Grey Moose we'd be coming back at any moment."

"Yes, but you'd have thought he'd have tried to help Grant and the girl."

"Oh no! Not Grey Moose!" said Harry decisively. "He must have backed out of more awkward situations and left more suckers to face the music than any man alive."

"But I thought this girl was in love with him?"

"So what?" shrugged Harry. "I guess there isn't much room for that stuff in Carl Kranston's life. But there was another thing to consider – he had to get that jewellery out of the country pronto! Just now it's white hot and sizzling! His pals had fallen down on the job, so it was up to him."

"It's tough on the girl," said Diana.

Harry stubbed out his cigarette. "Anybody who associates with Carl Kranston is asking for trouble, and she probably realises it better than most people. From what I hear, she's had a pretty good run with him. They've been around together for over five years."

The bus moved briskly along Fleet Street, where the traffic had dropped to a trickle. A few sub-editors were leaving their offices, with the last edition of their Sunday paper safely put to bed, and looking down they could see the lights in the basements of some of the large newspaper buildings. Diana imagined the throbbing of the presses sending a steady vibration through the entire structure. No doubt some of the stop press columns would contain a brief flash of that night's happenings in Mincing Lane.

"You seem to have found out quite a bit about Carl Kranston," she said presently.

"I have my spies," he grinned. "But it hasn't been any too easy. There's a lot of folk know *something* about Carl, but they're scared to hell to open their mouths."

"You never managed to get a photograph of him?"

Harry shook his head. "Carl Kranston is one of the few guys in this world who has never had his picture taken – not even on a bearskin rug."

"I wonder how he gets from one country to another without a passport," she speculated.

He half turned and grinned at her. "Have you ever recognised anyone from their passport photograph?" he asked.

"But surely if he's as high up as you seem to suspect, he'd had to have a photograph taken at some time or other."

"If he had, then the photographer didn't know he was taking Carl Kranston, and that name isn't attached to the picture."

"Oh, dear," sighed Diana. "It sounds terribly involved."

"Not a bit of it, when you take it a step at a time. A career like Carl Kranston's isn't built in a day, you know."

The bus rounded the corner of Trafalgar Square and sailed into Whitehall amidst the stragglers of the late theatre traffic. Under the passing glare of the overhead lights Diana looked much paler than usual, and she had obviously by no means recovered from her experience.

Suddenly she said, "I wonder what Kranston was going to do with me?"

To take her mind off that aspect of the business Harry interposed quickly, "I can't think how the Yard man lost you. He said you went into the office and he never saw you come out."

She wrinkled her forehead for a moment, then said, "I remember now ... I went down to the comps to correct some stuff on the stone, and I came out by the printers' entrance on the Embankment, instead of by the main hall. That's how he'd miss me."

"What happened then?"

"I'd just stepped out of the doorway when a man in a chauffeur's uniform came up and asked me if I was Diana

Stone. He said you'd sent him to fetch me on an urgent matter. Of course, I got in the car almost without thinking – and there was the Harrison girl pointing a revolver at me …"

"I see," said Harry slowly. "They'd figured all that out quite nicely."

"Maybe I should have taken a chance and screamed for help," Diana mused.

"It would have been a pretty slim chance," Harry told her. "I've no reason to doubt that she'd have been as good as her word. Still, if the chief had ordered 'em to bring you back alive maybe she'd only have hit you with the butt of the gun."

Diana shuddered.

"I'm sorry," said Harry. "You've had to put up with more than most girls could stand in one day. Let's forget it."

"But why should he want me 'bought back alive'?" Diana persisted with a faint smile.

"I wouldn't worry about that now," replied Harry. "Maybe he simply wanted to use you as a trump card in case he needed one. Or he may have thought that if I was chasing after you it would keep me from under his feet. Oh boy, he certainly made one mistake if he thought that!" he added reflectively.

She smiled.

"I was never so glad to see anybody in my life as I was to see you walk into that horrid cellar," she confessed.

"I certainly hope you'll go on being glad to see me," he said quietly as the bus jerked to a standstill outside Victoria Station. They peered down into a snack bar crowded with a strange assortment of humanity. Then the bus lurched on once more and round the corner past the Grosvenor Hotel.

"All the time I was in that car," went on Diana with a slight shiver, "I kept thinking, 'Things like this don't happen to people in broad daylight.' We passed several policemen, and once I caught my breath to cry out. But she guessed what was in my mind and poked the gun right up against me ..."

"You poor kid," sympathised Harry. "I'm surprised you didn't pass right out."

"I thought I was going to. But I dug my nails into my palms to stop myself. I thought there might be a chance of making a getaway when the car stopped. At least, I imagined I might scream and attract somebody's attention. But there was hardly a soul to be seen – it was Saturday lunchtime, and that part of the world was practically deserted."

"So they got you into the cellars without any trouble."

"I did manage to work the gag from my mouth and scream after I'd been tied up there for several hours. But that girl came in and replaced the gag." She rubbed her tender jawbone at the recollection of the incident.

The bus swayed over Ebury Bridge and swung round to the right through the purlieus of Pimlico. A small group of revellers came out of a public house, singing discordantly.

"Well, I hand it to you," said Harry admiringly. "You're pretty tough in that quiet way of yours. But I hope you won't have to face anything like that experience again."

They were silent for a minute or two as the bus wound its way into Sloane Square, where a brilliantly lighted coffee stall was doing a brisk trade.

"Harry," said Diana at length, "have you any idea who Grey Moose is?"

"I could make a near guess," he said, "but I won't. Tomorrow I expect to know for certain."

"Then you think you know his next move?"

"He has only two main interests at the moment," explained Harry. "First, to get that stuff out of the country; second, to get out himself. He can't risk making it a combined operation, in case he should be searched. Sir Richard is having all the ports carefully watched. So, as I see it, he'll try

204

to get the stuff out by the same method they've been using right from the start."

Noticing the gleam in his eyes and the eager set of his mouth, she caught his elbow for a moment and murmured, "Harry, don't stick your chin out too far."

He chuckled. "Leave it to me, honey. By the way," he added as a new thought struck him, "I thought you told me you carried a neat little .22 around. Have you got it with you today?"

She shook her head and looked down in her confusion. "I – I changed my handbag, and I must have forgotten it," she confessed.

The bus lurched to a standstill outside Chelsea Town Hall, and they climbed down the stairs and dismounted.

"There's no need to come any farther. I'll be perfectly all right now," she assured him, but he strode along beside her and insisted on accompanying her to her front door.

"How on earth will you get back to Sevenoaks at this time of night?" she asked in a worried tone.

"Quite simply. I'll hire a car from a fellow I know who runs a hire service," he told her.

"Will he be open at this time?"

"It's an all-night service, so there'll be no trouble."

"I could give you a shakedown on the settee in the lounge," she suggested as they turned out of the King's Road into the street where she lived.

"No, thanks," said Harry. "I must get back home tonight. It's very important."

"I'm afraid you're not going to get much sleep," she said.

"I guess an hour or two less beauty sleep can't make much difference to my ugly mug," he grinned.

At that moment they turned the corner as the road twisted at a fairly sharp angle, and Harry stopped dead. Less than twenty yards away was a large American saloon car drawn up to the kerb. The tail lamp was still on and he could see the rear number-plate quite clearly. It was undoubtedly his Columbia.

"Well, what d'you know about that!" he whistled.

"Is – is it –" began Diana.

"I'll say it is! And it's right outside your flat."

For a few moments they did not move.

"What are you going to do?" she whispered.

"You stay here," he said. "I'll go and take a look."

His hand closed over the Colt in his jacket pocket as he moved silently ahead of her towards the car. Then without warning he crossed the road and approached from the opposite pavement. When he came level with it, straining to see inside the vehicle, it appeared to be empty; he turned and walked back, finally re-crossing and walking right up to it. A street lamp a few yards away lit the interior sufficiently for him to confirm that it was empty and he beckoned to Diana to join him.

"What on earth's going on?" she asked in a low tone.

"That's what I want to find out."

"Do you think there's someone inside the flat?"

"Have you got your key?"

She shook her head. "I'm afraid I left that in my other handbag, too."

"In that case we'll have to ring. You stay down here – I'll do it."

He mounted the four steps from the pavement and rang the bell of Diana's flat. There was a long silence, and he rang again. Presently a light appeared in the entrance hall, and he could hear someone descending the stairs. He motioned to Diana to keep out of line with the door as the person inside fumbled with the catch. A moment later the door was carefully opened, and Mrs Bentley stood there, wearing a heavy woollen dressing-gown over a long nightdress. She recognised Harry almost at once.

"Mr Denver! Is anything the matter?"

"Sorry to drag you out of bed, Mrs Bentley. I've brought Miss Stone back."

"Thank God she's safe! But where is she?" the housekeeper cried.

"Just a minute, Mrs Bentley," Harry said quietly. "Have you had any visitors this evening?"

"Not a soul, sir."

"You didn't see this car out here arrive?" He indicated the Columbia.

"No, sir. I've been in the kitchen at the back all the evening."

Harry signalled to Diana to come up the steps. They all went inside and shut the door.

"Stay here while I go up to the flat and take a look round," he said to the two women. He left them talking rapidly in loud whispers, Diana explaining the events of the day to an open-mouthed Mrs Bentley, and went quietly up the stairs.

He made his way cautiously into the lounge, quickly switching on the light as soon as he was through the doorway. The room was empty and just as he had seen it on his previous visit. Methodically, he went through the other rooms, but they were all quite deserted, and he called to the women below to join him.

When Mrs Bentley suggested getting them some coffee he found himself agreeing, though he rarely drank coffee except under his own roof. But he was feeling a sudden reaction to the events of the day and decided that a hot drink would lift his spirits for the journey home.

He and Diana went into the lounge and switched on the electric fire. It was just after midnight by the electric clock on the mantelpiece.

While they waited for the coffee Harry paced restlessly up and down. "I can't think why he should dump my car outside your door of all places," he said, with a worried frown.

"It does seem strange," she had to admit. "Harry, you don't think he's somewhere around here now?"

"I'm fairly certain he isn't," he reassured her. "I've got reasons for saying so, but we won't go into them now – it's so darn late …" He stifled a yawn.

When Mrs Bentley brought the coffee he drained his cup almost at a gulp and announced that he must be going. He promised to telephone Diana in the morning as soon as he had any news and he made his way downstairs.

But he was still vaguely worried. He walked round the car and examined it carefully. It seemed exactly as he had left it in Mincing Lane. Finally, he opened the door somewhat gingerly, climbed in, and switched on the dashboard light. As he looked at the instruments he suddenly recalled that he had not checked his oil lately, and he wondered whether he would be all right for the return journey. Maybe Carl Kranston had driven the car quite a way, and in that case the oil would be low.

He got out, lifted the bonnet, and searched for the dipstick. The street lamp was only a few yards away, so he could see fairly well. He found the dipstick and was unscrewing the cap of the oil tank when he noticed an unfamiliar length of thin rubber-covered wire.

Harry pulled out his pocket torch and warily traced the wire to the back of the dashboard. It was connected to the self-starter button. The other end went to the car battery, then disappeared somewhere beneath the floorboards. For a minute or two Harry ferreted around, and presently he discovered a neat little oblong canister, with what was obviously a tiny detonator wired in series with the starter and battery.

One push of that starter button and the car and passengers would have been blown to fragments …

CHAPTER TWENTY-FIVE

Harry carefully disconnected the bomb and placed it on the rear seat of the car. It was now obvious why Carl Kranston had brought back the car to Diana's flat. He had guessed that Harry would take her home after her trying ordeal, and naturally he would use the car to return to Caldicott Manor. It was rather an obvious trick, when one thought about it, but it might easily have worked when one was tired and off guard; in fact, it almost had. Kranston would have taken that into account; he didn't miss much.

Harry was so immersed in disconnecting the bomb that he did not notice the front door of the house open.

Diana was calling down to him. "Harry – what's wrong?"

He straightened himself and pulled down the bonnet of the car. "Oh, just a little trouble getting her started," he replied casually.

"Has it been tampered with at all?" she inquired anxiously.

"No, no, I guess it'll be all right."

To add credibility to this he extricated the starting handle from under the seat and inserted it under the bonnet. As he did so, he consoled himself by the thought that if there were any more booby traps in the car at least he wouldn't be caught inside it. He found himself standing over a foot away from the end of the handle as he lifted it somewhat tentatively. But it was all right. The engine sprang into life immediately. He withdrew the handle and waved to Diana.

"Go to bed, honey," he called. "See you soon."

He climbed into the car, waved to her once more, and engaged first gear.

He sped along the deserted roads, passing only a very occasional vehicle, and was soon in the outer suburbs. It took him thirty-five minutes to get home.

He locked the car in the garage and made his way upstairs, where he set his alarm clock for four-thirty, calculating that he would get a good three hours' sleep.

But it seemed not more than three minutes later that the persistent buzzing of the alarm woke him.

Harry tiptoed downstairs, carrying his shoes, and went into the kitchen where he set his favourite coffee-pot on the stove. It was still quite dark outside.

He noted that a tray was already set for his morning coffee, and he went to the cupboard to fetch three extra cups.

At ten minutes to five there was a smart rap on the side door, and he opened it promptly. Four men were standing there, and he noted approvingly that they were all in plain-clothes.

"Morning, sir," a gruff voice said. "I'm Sergeant Huish – we had orders from the Yard to report here."

"Come in, Sergeant," Harry said. "There's just time for a cup of coffee before we start."

"Very nice of you, sir. A hot drink would be a help if we've got to wait around. It's nippy this morning."

"I hope there won't be much waiting," said Harry, leading them into the kitchen and pouring out the cups of coffee.

"We didn't get any instructions from the Yard, except that we were to come armed," said the Sergeant.

"I'm glad they suggested that," Harry said. "This guy we're after is a pretty desperate type. He's sure to be armed and he'll use his gun if he gets half a chance."

The Sergeant looked thoughtful. "In that case, sir, we don't want to take any more risks than we can help. The thing is to catch him by surprise."

"That's exactly what I'm hoping to do," nodded Harry, stirring his coffee. "I'm pretty certain he won't be expecting us, and he's almost sure to be on his own."

"I see, sir. Shall we take the car?"

Harry considered this for a moment, then decided against it. "Too risky," he murmured. "He might hear the car in the distance even if he didn't drive right up, and I don't want this bird scared off if we can possibly avoid it."

The Sergeant stroked his moustache with his forefinger. "Are you sure he won't hear us walking along the road, sir?" he speculated.

Harry's eyes travelled down to the large size boots worn by his three visitors. "We'll have to hope for the best, that's all," he sighed. "But we've got to be careful. Everything's dead quiet at this time of morning."

"You haven't told us yet where we're going, sir," the Sergeant reminded him.

"Oh, sorry," said Harry. "We're going just down the road – to the Kingfisher."

"You mean the place where the Yard man was murdered?"

"That's the place."

"We've had that pub under observation on and off for quite a while," Sergeant Huish observed. "I hadn't heard there was likely to be trouble there today – and at this time of the morning, too."

"I'm not so sure about it myself," Harry said candidly. "But I've a hunch you won't have had a wasted journey."

The Sergeant drank what remained of his coffee and set down his cup on the kitchen table. "Well, sir, we're ready when you are," he said.

"Right!" Harry felt in his coat pocket for his automatic, then fetched a light overcoat from the hall for the morning was chilly.

A watery moon was gliding through masses of cloud as they came out into the drive and moved off towards the front gates.

"Keep in the shadows as far as possible," instructed Harry.

They split up into two pairs, Harry and the Sergeant walking ahead at an even pace with no outward sign of hurry.

"How are we going to get in the place so early?" the Sergeant wanted to know. "And have you got a warrant?"

"We're not going inside the pub itself – at least, not as far as I know," Harry enlightened him. "So I guess we can ignore any little technicalities if we corner our bird."

"Do you know who he is?"

"I can make a pretty good guess, but maybe we'd better wait and see if I'm right."

On the eastern horizon there was a faint pink smudge heralding the dawn.

Just as the Kingfisher loomed up before them Sergeant Huish caught Harry's arm. "There's a car drawn up there," he said, indicating a car standing on the far side of the inn.

Cautiously they approached it from the opposite side of the road, their two colleagues a few yards in the rear. There was no sound to be heard except the snort of a horse in a distant meadow and the sleepy chirrup of a blackbird in the hedgerow. The Sergeant made signs to his men, and when he and Harry were just past the car they approached it simultaneously from all sides. The figure of a solitary occupant was almost immediately visible.

He was sitting in the driving seat with the window down, and seemed to be listening intently. When he saw the figures approaching out of the dusk he switched on a powerful torch.

"Good Lord, Harry! What on earth are you doing here at this unearthly hour?" said the familiar voice of Inspector Bowen.

"You practically took the words right out of my mouth," replied Harry quietly. Discovering Bowen like this was a complete surprise. There was a grim set to the Inspector's usually pleasant features, as if he were equally suspicious.

Harry was about to make a further remark when a sound overhead suddenly attracted their attention. All five men looked up instinctively.

"The first of the pigeons!" said Harry softly.

"Pigeons!" echoed Bowen.

"Come on!" said Harry briskly. "You'd better join us, Bowen – there's no time to be lost. And for God's sake don't slam that car door."

Bowen got out of the car as noiselessly as possible, and Harry led the way towards the pigeon cotes in a corner of the bowling green adjoining the small car park at the back of the inn. The men bent almost double and moved carefully under the cover of the hedge, for it was getting rapidly lighter.

When they were about ten yards from the pigeon cotes there was another violent flutter of wings as a pigeon shot upwards, circled two or three times, then headed unhesitatingly in a north-easterly direction. A chilly dawn breeze stirred the leaves of the privet hedge. One of the men trod upon a twig, which snapped loudly, and they all paused for some seconds before moving forward again. They were approaching the cotes from the blind side and Harry was hoping to get right up to them without being discovered.

As he came within arm's reach there was again the sound of fluttering wings and, after making a swift signal to his followers, Harry poked his head round the corner of the cote and said quietly: "Those are a fine lot of birds you've got there, Rymer."

Rymer dropped the cylinder he had just taken from his pocket and made a sudden movement towards his hip.

"Don't do that!" snapped Harry quickly, displaying his Colt automatic for the first time. Rymer dropped his hand with a helpless shrug.

"My God! It's Rymer!" exclaimed Bowen, coming into view at that moment.

Rymer looked at the little group of men that had fanned out to cut off his retreat, but still did not speak. Harry strolled over and picked up the cylinder that had fallen to the ground. It had a screw-top that unfastened quite easily. Harry tilted some highly polished rubies into his palm.

"Where's the rest of the stuff?" he asked.

Rymer motioned with his head towards the inside of the pigeon cotes.

"Get it!" ordered Harry.

Rymer looked round the little group once more, hesitated a moment, then turned to obey. Harry beckoned to the sergeant and Bowen to move in a little, and changed his position so that he could keep Rymer under observation. However, he had reckoned without the fact that although it was rapidly getting lighter, the inside of the cote was still very obscure from the point of view of anyone standing outside.

"I want all the stuff, mind," he called, and he could hear Rymer moving around, presumably collecting it together.

"This is going to cause a damned scandal," whispered Bowen to Harry, as they waited for Rymer to re-emerge. "A Yard man as the head of a gang of crooks – it's never been heard of before."

"Carl Kranston never lets little things like that worry him," said Harry grimly.

"How the devil has he managed to get away with it?" demanded the bewildered Bowen.

"I guess he won't get away with it much longer," shrugged Harry.

"But I can't think how he got inside the Yard to start with. It took me years …" Bowen was almost talking to himself now, as Harry moved a pace nearer the doorway.

A few seconds later they exchanged a glance and without speaking a word made for the door of the pigeon cote. Bowen snapped on his torch and flashed it round the gloomy interior, where half a dozen startled birds blinked at them and rustled their wings. The small attaché case and a number of cylinders lay on the floor just inside, but there was no sign of Inspector Rymer. The beam of the torch swept quickly round the wooden structure, which was surprisingly spacious, and finally settled on some decayed brickwork in a distant corner.

Harry hastened over to it at once.

"It's an old well," he whispered. As Bowen came up with the torch, they noticed that a rope ladder was fastened to a hook just below the rim of the brickwork.

"So that's how he comes and goes," said Harry, preparing to descend the ladder. "It must lead to some underground passage – this district seems to be honeycombed with 'em!"

"Wait," said Bowen. "He's sure to be armed."

"Of course he's armed – but he's mainly interested in making his getaway, not stopping to fight it out," said Harry, swinging a leg over and placing his foot on the top rung of the ladder.

"Where will the passage lead?" asked Bowen.

Harry paused. "It may come out in the pub somewhere – or it may link up with White Towers. Better send a couple of men to each place as quickly as possible. Those going to White Towers had better use your car."

Bowen turned and rapped out the orders without wasting any time, but Harry was almost down to the foot of the rope ladder when he was ready to follow. Bowen realised that the ladder would probably not take the weight of two at the same time, so he waited until Harry had reached the bottom of the well before he stepped on the top rung.

"All right, Bowen," called Harry. "Make it snappy!"

Bowen came clambering down two rungs at a time. It was only about a twelve-foot ladder, which ended about two feet above the well bottom.

"Any sign of him?" asked Bowen, as he stepped off the ladder, breathing quickly.

"Not yet," said Harry. "Keep that torch down and hold it away from you."

The tunnel they were in led in one direction only – towards the inn. It was narrower and lower than the one between the inn and White Lodge, and at times Bowen stooped considerably as he led the way, all too slowly for Harry's liking. But Bowen was still obviously expecting an ambush of some sort, and had decided to take as few risks as possible. He knew from his Yard experience that Rymer could be a very awkward customer in a tight corner. He recalled taking part in a Soho raid when Rymer had dealt with a couple of young Greeks in a manner which Bowen had considered unnecessarily tough.

But there was still no sign of Carl Kranston alias Inspector Rymer. When they had progressed about forty yards there was a sudden bend in the tunnel and as they came up to it Bowen hesitated once again.

"Any idea where we are?" he whispered to Harry, who was almost treading on his heels.

"Haven't a clue," Harry replied, somewhat impatient at the delay. "Wait a minute though. Shine the torch along to the right … further …"

They edged round the corner, following the beam of light. A second later they saw the foot of a flight of steps which Harry recognised as those leading up to the inn and emerging behind the club room wall. He remembered that when he had climbed those steps with Diana he had noticed that the tunnel continued beyond them, but they had not had the opportunity to explore further.

"What now?" asked Bowen.

Harry sized up the situation rapidly. If Rymer had gone up the stairs and out by way of the club room the men up there would most likely have picked him up. He would probably foresee this and prefer to take a long chance of getting through to White Towers before his retreat could be cut off there.

"This way," said Harry, ignoring the stairs and moving off quickly along the tunnel towards White Towers. "Put your torch out; I'll use mine." He produced his pencil torch which gave less light, but quite sufficient for their purpose, and they hurried along the tunnel towards the lift shaft. Harry led the way down the incline at a brisk pace and did not slacken until he judged they were within twenty yards of their objective.

A distant sound like a persistent hammering made Harry stop for a moment.

He turned to Bowen and said quietly, "Sounds to me as if the door of the lift has jammed."

Even as he spoke the hammering noise stopped and they heard Rymer's rasping command: "Get back or I shall shoot!"

Harry switched off the torch at once.

"My God! We've got him," breathed Bowen, clicking the safety catch of his revolver, and every nerve tensed.

"Flat against the wall," Harry whispered to Bowen. But even as they took up position, a blinding beam of light from a powerful torch dazzled them.

"Back – back to the end of the tunnel!" snapped Rymer.

"Take it easy, Rymer," said Harry. "There are men waiting there, even if you got past us. You'll never get away."

"Shut up, damn you!"

A loud report echoed through the tunnel and a bullet whistled past Harry's head. He realised that Rymer was not particular whether they retreated or were disposed of by some other alternative – in fact, he would probably prefer them

218

dead so that there would be less chance of their hampering his escape from the country. He was snapping the torch on and off, and during the split second of its dazzling light was firing at anything he saw. Bowen had taken cover against the opposite wall of the tunnel a little farther back, and the next time the light flicked on Harry aimed just above it and fired twice in return, but the light came on again a few seconds later and was followed by more shots.

The next time the light jerked on Harry and Bowen fired simultaneously and Harry also saw the flash of Rymer's revolver. The explosions reverberated through the tunnel and the echoes had not died before they were submerged by an ominous rumble from above their heads.

"Get back!" cried Bowen, grabbing Harry's arm. "The roof … the roof's caving in …"

What caused the collapse of the roof they never discovered. It might have been the displacement of a stone by one of the bullets which started the landslide; a landslide that seemed to grow in proportion every second. Harry and Bowen took to their heels and ran blindly back the way they had come. Twice they slipped on the slimy flagstones, recovered, and stumbled on. The roar of falling stones echoed behind them as they reached the steps that led into the club room, and it was only when they reached the top that they paused for breath.

"Looks as if the whole tunnel has caved in!" gasped Bowen.

"There's one thing about it," panted Harry. "He'll never get out this way. Come on, Bowen, let's get down to White Towers as quickly as we can make it."

CHAPTER TWENTY-SIX

Harry selected a particularly attractive mayfly, attached it to his line and skimmed it expertly across the still waters of the pond. Diana tried to wriggle into a more comfortable position on her camp stool without much success and rubbed a tingling gnat-bite on her ankle. She glanced at her wristwatch for the twelfth time.

"How much longer do we have to stay here, Harry?" she inquired, trying not to sound too bored.

"Why, all day, of course," replied Harry. "The fish'll be biting any minute now …"

"And then am I supposed to cook them over a wood fire?"

Harry laughed. "Heck, no! There's a whole basketful of food and drink in the back of the car."

This information cheered her slightly, but a few minutes later she found herself looking at her watch again. It was just a quarter to eleven. They had already been sitting beside this deserted pond for nearly two hours without a fish as much as raising its nose above the surface.

"Gee, can't you feel this sun soaking into the pores?" enthused Harry. "I guess this is just what the doctor ordered."

"Don't you find it a bit dull – I mean when the fish aren't biting?" said Diana.

"Not a dull moment," he assured her cheerfully.

"But you've got such an active brain, Harry."

"Even the most active brain needs to relax some time," he informed her. "Besides, I'm a lazy guy at heart. Just sitting around, that's the life for me, I guess."

"Oh no it isn't," she contradicted. "You're just in that sort of mood. It's a reaction from all the excitement you've been through lately."

Harry looked up at her and grinned. "Certainly was exciting," he agreed.

They sat watching his float for a few moments without speaking, each busy with their thoughts of the events of the past few weeks.

"That was pretty smart of you to find out about those pigeons being used to get the stuff out of the country," she murmured.

"Yes." He nodded. "I'd often seem 'em circling round the Kingfisher, and I asked the landlord about them once or twice. He told me about the races you hold over here – it was all new to me, so I was kinda interested. Maybe that's why it stuck in my mind, and when you'd overheard 'em say: 'Release at dawn', something went click. By the way, I forgot to tell you, I heard from Sir Richard this morning that Hood was at the receiving end. The police were on the watch in all the cities where he has his undercover business. The two pigeons that got away came down in Brussels, and Hood's agent was caught red-handed taking off the cylinders."

"But of course they didn't get Hood," she said.

"Well, it means his Brussels place closes down from now on, and he daren't show his face in Belgium anyhow," said Harry cheerfully. "It's only a matter of time before these guys make a slip."

"Maybe you'll make one yourself one of these days, Harry," she observed softly.

Harry laughed. "Maybe I will. But why worry about that on a lovely morning?"

A large pike came to the surface in the centre of the pond and promptly went to sleep in the morning sunlight.

"There – why don't you catch that one?" cried Diana excitedly.

Harry shook his head. "I guess he's had more than enough food for the next few hours. Besides, I never was partial to pike."

"Weren't you a bit suspicious of Inspector Bowen when he turned up that morning?" she asked presently.

"It did give me a start for a moment," he admitted. "Simply because I couldn't altogether leave Bowen out of my list of suspects: and Bowen was in the room that morning Sam Crawford took the poison – he actually had access to that flask. What was more, he knew you were Falconer's sister. All the same, I'd known Bowen for quite a while, and he didn't seem right for the part of Grey Moose. He'd told me stories of his days with the county constabularies, and they seemed genuine enough. When I heard that pigeon go up from the back of the pub, I was pretty sure Bowen wasn't our man."

"It could have been released by an associate," she suggested.

"Except that, as far as we knew, Grey Moose's organisation had been reduced to one man – Grey Moose himself."

"He could have roped in someone to do the dirty work," she pointed out. "He's been rather good at that in the past."

"You think of everything," grinned Harry, drawing in his line and casting it in a new direction. "Anyhow, Rymer didn't bother to deny anything when we caught him with the stuff."

"You're very lucky to have got out of that tunnel alive," said Diana, with a slight shudder. She hesitated a moment, then asked: "Have they found anything down there yet?"

"Nothing except a piece of an old Roman drinking vessel that would have delighted the heart of poor Mr Dancey," replied Harry.

"Poor old Dancey," she murmured. "It's a shame he didn't live to see the end of Carl Kranston."

Harry laid down his rod for a moment to light a cigarette.

"I'm not so sure we've seen the end of Carl Kranston," he said quietly.

"But I thought you said the tunnel had caved in for over thirty yards …"

"The fact remains that they haven't yet found Carl's body."

"But how could he have possibly got out?"

Harry shrugged. "He might have got the lift to work somehow, even climbed the lift shaft. He might even have escaped by another tunnel beyond the lift and sealed it up after him. One thing's certain, anyway – if he did get away, he's out of the country by this time, and we shan't see any more of him for quite a while."

"Well, that's a relief anyway."

"You know, we were darn lucky that day when we discovered the lift," Harry told her. "It was still at the bottom, in the tunnel, waiting to take us up again. But if that butler fellow or someone had happened to call it up while we were in the tunnel we'd have been in real trouble. Apparently it could be worked from either end by those who knew the secret, but we wouldn't have known how."

"Yes, you're right," Diana agreed. "Now you come to mention it, Harry, I can't quite see why the lift was at the top of the shaft when we discovered it. Surely, if Grant and the girl had gone down, it should have been in the tunnel ready to take them up again?"

Harry chuckled. "Yeah, I dare say it would have been if you hadn't started fooling around with that little statue and caused it to come up."

Diana looked at her watch again and wondered how soon she dare suggest they should begin lunch. "I expect Sir Richard's pleased. I'm surprised he didn't offer to put you on the permanent strength at the Yard."

"He knew better than that."

Diana scratched another gnat-bite on her right ankle. "It was certainly an amazing achievement on Kranston's part to

223

get into Scotland Yard. Have they found out exactly how he managed it?" she inquired.

"Actually, it was comparatively straightforward," Harry told her. "Carl simply murdered the real Rymer, who was being sent by the South African police to London to clear up a diamond smuggling case, and assumed his identity. After that, he got special permission to stay on and study Scotland Yard methods."

"But surely there was a body?" queried Diana.

"Oh, yes, a body went overboard all right. But it was supposed to be that of a Mr Marcus Soden, which was Carl's name on the ship's passenger register. As it happened on the first night out, hardly anybody knew anyone else, and it was comparatively easy for Carl to slip into the dead man's shoes."

Diana made a futile dab at a threatening fly and changed her position on the camp stool.

"How did you get to hear all this?" she asked.

"We eventually persuaded Doctor Grant to talk."

"And the girl?"

"She wouldn't say a word."

"She's still in love with him, of course."

"Love's a wonderful thing when it makes a woman hold her tongue," said Harry thoughtfully.

"Are you hinting that our chatter is frightening away the fish?" she suggested.

"Well, they're certainly not biting," he smiled.

"We've not scared the old pike – he's still fast asleep," she reminded him, indicating that ancient placidly floating on the surface of the pond.

"Why not let me have a go?" she suggested.

Harry looked surprised.

"But – but you don't want to fish, do you?" he stammered.

"At least it's better than doing nothing," she replied gravely. "Besides, it'll be something to write about in my column."

"Well," he said, somewhat grudgingly handing over the rod, "I guess it can't do much harm if you hold it for a few minutes."

"Thank you, Harry," she smiled sweetly. "I'll take great care of it."

"Keep your hand steady," he advised, watching her closely.

"Wouldn't it seem more natural if the fly at the end of the line moved around a bit?" she suggested. "Otherwise, it's pretty dull for everybody."

"No, no, it won't do at all," he said, so anxiously that she sat perfectly still and obeyed his instructions. Presently, she said quietly: "When are you going back to America, Harry?"

"Did I say anything about going back?" he demanded in some surprise.

"Well, no, but it's your home, isn't it?"

"I guess so, but I like it here, too. I can relax here." He blew out a leisurely stream of smoke from his cigarette.

"There's more money to be made over there, of course," she ventured.

"Who cares about money? I get by all right!"

"I'm afraid you won't make much out of the fish you catch. And the States must be much more exciting …"

Harry eased himself on his haunches and looked at her with a puzzled frown.

"Say, are you trying to tell me I've outstayed my welcome?" he demanded.

She laughed.

"Of course not, Harry. I just thought that perhaps some nice American girl was patiently waiting for you."

"You don't know much about our girls if you think they wait patiently. No, there's nothing like that. As a matter of fact, I've been seriously thinking of settling down here. I like this part of the world – it suits me. The fishing's okay, and a guy can take time off to think."

"That's true," she nodded. "You've a lovely old house and a perfect butler. What more could a man want?"

Harry shifted his feet awkwardly, plucked a blade of grass, and looked frankly worried.

"I guess there is something else," he said at last.

"Oh?" murmured Diana absently, her eyes on the float. "What's that?"

"It's a woman," he blurted out. "I thought maybe you and me, Diana. I thought …"

"Yes?" said Diana, rubbing yet another gnat-bite just below her knee.

"Well," continued Harry desperately, "you've often said how you like the old manor, and you're crazy about Miles, and I thought maybe in time you could get around to letting me keep an eye on you, just in case Carl Kranston came back and –"

"Harry!" she cried with sudden fervour.

"Yes?" he responded, eagerly stumbling to his feet.

"Harry! Look! I believe I've got a bite!"

THE END

Printed in Great Britain
by Amazon